Lacey
Leighton

Ruth Jones

Cover design by Ruth Jones© 2017
Page Layout by Steven Weaver

Silver Wolf Press

ISBN:978-0-9986990-0-4

Library of Congress Control Number: 2017904168

For Chris, Kenai,

and Marie

CONTENTS

LACEY LEIGHTON

PART I SURROUNDINGS

CHAPTER 1

FAMILY

We've all had that day when we awoke from a sound sleep knowing something big was going to happen. For this child, this was that day, and it had been in her thoughts all week. As she was climbing out of bed, a faint smile crept across her face, and when she became aware of this incipient joy, the smile grew stronger.

How long had it been since she had cause to smile? She couldn't remember. Smiles were not abundant in this house; joy was non-existent.

What she didn't know, couldn't have known, was how much this glorious day's adventure would forever change her life.

Quickly eating her breakfast porridge, she got up from the well-worn table, washed her spoon and bowl, and immediately went to her bedroom. Opening the door she walked slowly to the dresser. She hesitated, drew a quite breath, and opened the bottom dresser drawer.

Looking at the neatly folded clothes temporarily erased the smile that had been there since she awoke that morning. Two drab cotton dresses stared back at her. One was an odd color – light blue with dark blue trim. It wasn't so much blue as a muted gray with a tinge of blue, and the material was especially course to the touch. Sitting in Church on Sunday, this dress always irritated her tender skin. The other dress was for school and the material was softer. But that advantage was overshadowed by the color – dull and monotonous beige.

On this special day, she wanted to get dressed up, to be pretty. Wearing her overalls felt clumsy, while her dresses felt freer. They had a certain flow – a touch of femininity.

Of course she was only twelve years old, soon to be thirteen, and had no way of knowing the future shock to come. Corsets!

Her mother had died when she was born, and besides Papa, her only siblings were two older brothers who rarely gave her notice.

She grew up knowing very little of her mother, as Papa rarely mentioned her. A quick and gruff growl, or perhaps a stinging slap to the cheek, stopped any inquiry.

Never knowing this woman caused a profound emptiness in her heart. She often wondered what her mother had been like, and how different her own life may have been if her mother had lived. Had she been a kind person? She wanted her to be. Would she have doted on her only daughter? Yes, assuredly. Would she have protected her daughter from Papa's erratic behavior?

Not sure she could have.

All this pondering, she knew, served no purpose.

And there was no doubt as to her future existence – she'd be working the farm for Papa, or someone else.

Papa had been wounded in the war during the battle of Cross Keys in Rockingham County, Virginia on June 8, 1862, and since has had to depend on his children and sympathetic neighbors to help care for the small farm that fed them. He was a bitter man, always was. One of those arrogant sorts that thought life owed him. His life had been difficult, this was true, and it left a scar so deep that the chasm was impossible to negotiate.

The story of his battle scars were recounted time and time again, until his children could recite the story perfectly.

They understood well that Confederate Army Major General Thomas J. "Stonewall" Jackson advanced fifty-eight hundred Confederates against eleven thousand Union soldiers. Though they were outnumbered, the Confederates won that battle, and Union forces retreated.

Losses and casualties were high on both sides.

Papa had been on the losing side. He was no confederate. He wasn't so much opposed to slavery as much as he was against those Rebs thinking they could leave the Union without harsh penalty. He'd gone to the meetings in town that revved up the war machine, and when he was able, he enlisted.

Anything would be better than being at home.

After only a few weeks away from his family, this soldier decided that if he survived the war, he'd leave his wife and children, and head west.

On the day of the Cross Keys battle, luck was with

Papa. A large downed tree trunk hid him well; it was spring, and a tangle of branches with many large leaves added to his security. He wasn't particularly a brave man, but you couldn't call him a coward either. Whatever the circumstance, he'd muster up the courage, or perhaps it was gall, to get through any situation.

His fellow soldiers of the Forty-second Pennsylvania Volunteer Infantry were to his left, and quite a distance away. How that happened he didn't know, and through careful consideration believed he was safer staying with the downed tree.

As he was eyeing the enemy across the battle field, he noticed an impressive figure, though his horse was unimpressive – stocky and certainly not a beauty. He expected the rider to mount a stallion, not a Morgan.

Quite a performance Papa mused as he observed the soldier posturing with true elegance, and with a sense of invulnerability.

There was something familiar about the rider. Suddenly, Papa recognized "Stonewall" Jackson! The Major General had been pointed out to him once, before the war, and there he was, in perfect line of sight for Papa's rifle.

Taking aim, Papa noticed the LeMat pistol sitting idly in Jackson's holster. It was a nine shot revolver designed by a Dr. LeMat in New Orleans in 1861. Papa's only interest was collecting guns and rifles, and he had been told that the LeMat pistol was Jackson's "weapon of choice."

It was an innovative weapon which was used by the

Confederates, not the Union, and Papa was captivated. When he realized this distraction, it was too late, and "Stonewall" was out of range.

Papa's moment to be a hero was gone.

He then hoped by changing positions he could spot the General once more, take aim, and find his glory. Instead, as soon as he moved out of his sheltered stance, Papa was hit with a round piece of metal that came soaring at him, tearing his arm to shreds. The brutal speed and power of that projectile knocked him off his feet as his leg got caught inside a cavern in that downed tree. The pain was excruciating and the leg was broken.

The veins in Papa's neck always fluctuated madly as he recalled, too vividly, the memory of that day. When he started telling his story (and it was recounted often), he'd be sitting down, typically at the table. And by the story's end, he'd have stood up, beads of sweat forming on his upper lip, and he'd be swinging his arm in full abandon as he recounted the confederates' victories – and his own losses.

The Cross Keys battle, like the other battles fought in the Shenandoah, left that luscious green valley red with death. Papa brought back to his house, to his family, that horrendous site, in all its violent and gruesome detail.

War changes people. The change for many is to a higher character, but for this soldier, the war imprinted a more calloused and crueler nature.

Besides his war ramblings, the girl and her brothers heard from Papa on the hardships he endured in his childhood and youth, with a mix of truths and untruths.

Her Heritage! She knew what that meant, even at her tender age, and felt the pain of it. This was a bright, alert and sensitive child and if you watched and observed Papa, you'd have to consider that this child's nature must have been inherited from the mother's side.

She abhorred the stories her papa divulged in his drunken stupors of self-pity. Yet the stories offered the child a perspective on his true nature. Even at her young age she understood that Papa was not a good and decent father, and this understanding allowed for a sense of power over her grim circumstances.

Hearing Papa's voice downstairs, she was reminded of that heritage, that legacy. She heard him barking to her eldest brother in his usual combative tone.

"You should be thankful that you have the life that I give you! My father was not at all considerate of his wife and children or their circumstances. Be grateful!"

Papa never once mentioned his father by name – so telling of his attitude towards his father.

Whatever good experiences Papa may have had as a result of his mother's love didn't carry through to good behavior with his own wife and children.

To the contrary, he simply continued the bad behavior of his own father.

* * * * * *

Grandfather (Papa's father) had been a farrier, trimming and balancing horse's hooves for the purpose of shoeing. He had worked for the town's blacksmith for a couple of years and seemed to have the patience needed to learn some of the blacksmith's skills: fabricating, adapting, and adjusting the metal shoes. The blacksmith was so impressed by the farrier's ease of learning that he hoped one day to teach him how to fabricate and repair tools, and the forging of architectural pieces and the like.

Learning had always come easy to this farrier. And perhaps that is why he typically became bored and wanted to move on. Nonetheless, the farrier did have grandiose ideas and filled his days through notions and dreams of working for himself, of being his own boss where his patience wouldn't be tested. His temper and nature inevitably ruined his first chance to do just that.

And that chance came in the form of a landowner from a nearby town. While visiting, his horse threw a shoe. As he was dismounting from his mare, a baker from the bread shop across the street was walking past, and told the landowner of the local foundry.

As his horse was shoed, the landowner noticed the skills the farrier possessed, and the next week he was back, talking to the farrier. He explained that the blacksmith, in his town, had died from a gunshot wound received from a duel while defending his wife's honor.

Speculation was that he died in vain.

The landowner's town needed a blacksmith and was having difficulty finding one; the landowner decided that this farrier could be the answer. This farrier didn't own the foundry; he was merely a worker. In time, the landowner believed, the farrier would become an expert blacksmith.

So the deal was struck, and the foundry re-opened three months later.

The farrier had moved himself and his family to a small residence attached to the foundry. It was a hovel, really. The deceased blacksmith had lived in a cottage on the outskirts of town, and his widow and her children still lived there.

The new farrier was to run the business, collect all fees, pay all bills, learn the trade, and remit a minimal sum for the use of the foundry to the widow's eldest son who now owned the building that housed the foundry. In exchange, the small residence was rent free. Once the farrier learned the blacksmith trade, therefore increasing revenue, the widow and her eldest son presumed he would find other lodgings.

For a short while all went well, and the town was pleased with their decision. Unfortunately, all wasn't well with the farrier.

This was an inherently lazy man, a self-righteous man who wanted the glory without the hard work. What monies he did acquire from his work, he hoarded, giving his family only the barest of necessities.

His daily chores, including the shoeing and the financial accounting, fell behind. He knew there was no rush in getting these things done. He'll get to it, eventually.

The widow had complained often to the landowner that the weekly remittance hadn't been paid.

Everyone in the town noticed there were problems. Not only had the business been run down, but also, there was no evidence that the farrier had any intention of learning more of the trade.

Enough was enough and the town folk, the widow and her son told the landowner that this farrier must go. Not only was he taking advantage of the good people of this town, he was also mistreating his own family which they could not tolerate. One observer had witnessed the farrier hitting his son with a horse crop several times, right across the child's back.

The landowner recognized everyone's concern, but also knew they needed a farrier. Could the farrier be reasoned with? Could he discuss these issues? He hoped the farrier was a reasonable man.

It was this discussion, if you can call it a discussion, which changed the landowner forever. This was a rational and honorable man who believed that all livings souls attempted, under decent circumstances, to charitably value another's disquiet. He knew this to be true of himself, and he naturally projected this onto others – a bit naïve perhaps. And, this principle became shattered at the hands of a man incapable of altruism.

It was a bright sunny day, following several days of spring showers. Summer was coming and the scent of honeysuckle was strong. It was barely past ten o'clock in the morning as the landowner walked into the foundry and eyed the farrier lazing inside the door.

"Good Morning," he uttered reluctantly, receiving no response. He was appalled when he saw the amount of horse dung piled in the corner. The fire pit was cold and the one and only horse was only partially shoed.

The landowner snapped loudly, "Good Morning," and nudged the farrier's tattered boot in order to get his attention. He knew the farrier must have some idea as to why he was there.

And he did.

The farrier suddenly jumped up in a rage yelling and swinging an axe. It happened so quickly and so unexpectedly that the landowner fell backwards trying to get out of the foundry, catching his foot on an iron anvil placed just inside the door.

"You think you can come in here to bark orders. You know nothing. Get out of here before I wield this axe in your direction."

Grinning despicably, the farrier continued spewing his poison. The landowner was so horrified that he didn't even feel or notice his broken ankle until he was out the door and tried to stand. He crawled away praying not to feel the sharp blade of that axe on his flesh.

How could he have so utterly misjudged this man?

Several people came to his aid and pulled him to safety. Yet, in spite of being out of harm's way, the landowner couldn't stop shaking. This was the life altering experience that changed forever what the landowner once considered to be tried and true – persistent optimism in the face of humanity.

That belief was now set ablaze and charred to ashes.

The town's Constable, a hefty fellow with an unkempt long beard and mustache, was contacted immediately. As instructed, the Constable threw the farrier out of the foundry.

Later that day, it was difficult to watch the farrier's wife and children walk down the street, in shame and despair, with their heads covered and lowered, carrying but a few wares.

It was a pitiful sight.

The boy seemed to be the most affected and afflicted – one minute clinging to his mother, and the next defiantly holding his head high. He'd peer at the town folk now in the street, with a piercing cold gaze unexpected in such a young child. The effects of this day would haunt this child with rage and relentless penalties for the rest of his life.

The boy's father, the farrier, abandoned his family immediately following the Constable's indignation. And the mother and her children, now penniless, were walking down the street not knowing where they were going, never to see the farrier again.

* * * * * *

The boy grew up fast. The chip on his shoulder was a constant companion. How could it not be? But he did survive.

His mother and her children moved from town to town, finding work in the fields, finding work anywhere. When he was eleven, he lost his sister to disease, and his mother died a few years later, probably from exhaustion.

The boy wandered.

He grew into a fine-looking fellow, slender with transparent blue eyes that cut to the core of one's being. His brown curly hair only added to his mystique. He was handsome and he knew it. It was part of his charm some say. The young ladies wanted to be his, regardless of a rough and raw edge that could be alarming.

He was a quick learner, sharp, and he'd rather use his brain than his brawn. Nonetheless, he was moody, temperamental, and he was fired from several jobs.

Eventually, he found work as a clerk in a law office. Now, he thought, he'd get the life he deserved and went after it. It didn't take him long to meet the right young lady that suited his needs.

Long ago he decided on the "type" he'd marry: pretty, petite, light eyes, and hair color didn't matter.

Most importantly, she'd abide by his rules.

No backtalk!

And if he was patient he'd find the one arriving to the marriage with a substantial dowry, business, or land.

A year later he met a farmer's daughter. She was hesitant to marry, but before long he convinced her that any reservations were unfounded. Her mother and father had both died the year before, only months apart, and, as the only child with no relatives, she inherited the farm and received a small annual stipend. Her new husband had no intention of working the farm and she agreed to lease it out.

With the monies from the lease, her stipend, and his clerk wages, they could get by. They were able to rent a bungalow in a nearby town.

A year after getting married, a son was born, and another boy the following year. Life wasn't easy, but she tolerated this existence as best she could. If choosing again was an option, she knew she wouldn't marry him.

He was a bully, arrogant and intolerant.

Settling in, and daily routine preserved her sanity.

Then news of war – devastating! It was impossible to grasp.

He told her he enlisted because it was his duty, and that he'd be going to a battle, somewhere soon. A few weeks later, the leased farm was vacated, and the decision was made for her to go to the farm with the boys and wait out the war. She knew how to work it well enough to feed herself and the boys. They would all move back to town once he returned.

He did return less than six months after leaving, but was maimed. His right arm had been amputated, and his broken leg never mended well, leaving a decisive limp. Working as a clerk now would be impossible.

With the war, leasing the land was no longer feasible, and for him, now having to work the farm, proved arduous. For a short while, the farm was a sanctuary of sorts. But the anger and resentment he felt stewed within him, affecting all aspects of life.

Since the young boys weren't old enough to work the fields or carry the water from the well, these tasks fell to his wife and himself. Between them, they were able to eke out their meager existence. The one thing Papa was grateful for was that his wife had bought an old nag from a family whose son had been killed in the war, and now that old nag brought needed relief.

A couple of years after he returned home from the war his wife gave birth to a little girl – the delivery was difficult and his wife died during childbirth. Her daily fatigue, the neighbors believed, brought her easily to death's door.

He became embittered, not because he lost his wife, but now, he, alone, had to raise and feed these three children.

CHAPTER 2

THE CHILD

This child never knew an easy day. Up at dawn, farm work, school, more farm work, cooking. Life was difficult for all in this family.

Papa had firmly believed that sending his children to school was nonsense, but the Church Elders insisted that he do the right thing.

Begrudgingly, he allowed his children to attend the one room school house on the outskirts of town for the two hours of teaching the ABC's – even the girl attended, who also learned skills helpful to a farm girl.

After a disheartening inspection of her dresses, the girl remembered the big wooden trunk in the attic, with her mother's clothes and forgotten memorabilia. Perhaps a suitable dress was waiting in that trunk for her to wear today. She climbed the rickety wooden stairs attached to the outside of the house that led to the garret. Opening the door, she sneezed and coughed as the dust, dirt and spider webs were shaken loose.

The family rarely went up here. The brothers had no

reason to venture up to that musty room, and Papa's leg prevented him from climbing the stairs regularly. And, the girl avoided the attic because it's where her papa kept his "imposing, revered and celebrated" guns and war mementos.

And besides, seeing Mother's trunk, that housed long forgotten possessions and memories, only made the child's desolate situation that much harder to bear.

Entering the dark windowless space, she lit the oil lamp that was sitting next to the door on a tiny table, and carefully surveyed the room before going forward. The floor wasn't to be relied upon. One slip and you could find yourself falling through the floor, landing down below. She inched slowly towards her mother's possessions and hoped that there would be something in that sturdy trunk that she could alter and wear.

Her mother was petite; the girl was not. She was tall and slender for her age, with her father's curly brown hair and her mother's deep serene green eyes. People have said that she was a beauty even at her young age – a natural beauty, as was her mother.

Learning to sew in school, she could alter one of her mother's dresses to fit an "almost" thirteen year old. She opened the trunk and right on top sat two dresses. The dresses weren't softer than hers, yet the yellow and pink colors were brighter.

Basting the yellow dress, she pulled it over her head and tied the sash. With no breasts, no hips, and a torso shaped liked a ruler, the dress hung pitifully.

More tailoring was necessary.

To put that much work into a dress she didn't like, was a waste of time. She should clearly wear one of her own dresses. But wait. Maybe there are more dresses in the trunk, she pondered for a moment.

Taking off the yellow dress, she walked back to her mother's wares, and started pulling out items from the trunk: hairbrushes, hairpins, two sets of gloves, a photograph of an old woman and another photograph of a young child (they both appeared to be asleep, but they were lifeless.)

Also in the trunk was a diary.

She eyed the diary for several minutes.

What did her mother have to say? Would reading it be wrong? These were her mother's private feelings, private words. Did she have a right to invade these memories? She sat the diary down next to the stairs and wondered if she would ever read it.

Going back to the trunk, she spotted a dash of color peeking through another set of gloves. She cleared away a bible, another photograph, and tugged at the material underneath. It was stuck on a nail, or something else, and she stopped pulling. Actually, one of the buttons on the material was caught underneath a baby rattle that had become wedged in between a photo frame and a broken plat from the underside of the chest. After gently sorting out the infringing items, she took the rattle in her hand. Could she feel her mother's touch in the rattle? Tears swelled in her eyes, and abruptly, she shook off that emotion.

It did her no good to think of these things.

The material was now free, and it was a fine-looking sage-green dress. Green was this child's favorite color and she wondered where her mother would have worn this dress. It could have been for Church, she supposed, but it was too handsome a dress for that occasion. And obviously, it wasn't for working the farm.

The dress, she knew, was made from silk. She saw this luxurious material once before when the Deacon's wife died, and was buried in a pale blue silk dress with elaborate needlepoint around the neck.

That was the first chance she had to see a lifeless body in a coffin, a sight that gave her chills at each recollection. The funeral was disturbing, and the contrasted prettiness of the dress was unsettling.

She examined her mother's dress and believed that with alterations, it might work for her outing. Closing the trunk she vowed to re-visit this place, and perhaps to connect with her mother. She had never been ready to venture into this part of her life, but today was different.

Today she was inspired.

Carefully putting back into the trunk all the bits and pieces belonging to her mother, she tenderly closed the lid. She realized she had been staring at the closed lid for several minutes. How different her life may have been if her mother had lived.

Now, all she had was this trunk full of memories.

Now, all she had was this tiresome life.

Now, all she wanted to do was cry.

Her face slackened as she saw the days ahead.

Examining her mother's dress put a slight smile back

on her face. Then gingerly she crossed the attic floor, where she knelt to pick up the diary.

As she was climbing down the stairs she could hear Papa coming back from town riding Ole Jessie who was snorting with every step. She quickly climbed down the stairs, ran around to the front door, entered the farmhouse, and hurried to her room.

At this point, she was unsure as to whether or not Papa would allow her to alter and wear the dress, let alone read the diary. She wondered if he ever read the diary, and decided most likely he hadn't, simply because he had no interest.

She decided to tell Papa that she found the dress, but not that she found the diary.

How bold she had become.

He came through the front door as she entered the kitchen to get the sewing kit. To aid in her request, she asked Papa if he'd like something to drink or perhaps a snack. When he shook his head no, she mentioned the dress, and didn't tell the whole truth. Not letting him know she was in the attic was important. So she lied.

"Papa, I just found this dress of Mother's. I was looking through some old boxes from underneath my bed and found the dress crumpled beside a pair of my overalls. I would like to sew it to fit me, so I can wear it today. Is that alright?"

She awaited the barrage of disapproval.

On the contrary, Papa said yes! And he said yes with no hesitation. She wasn't sure she heard correctly.

This was the week of surprises.

He was allowing her to miss one day of school and most of the daily chores in order to go to the bazaar, and he actually promised to give her some spare change. And now he's letting her keep the dress!

Was she wrong about him?

She ran to her room, sat on her bed and picked up the needle and thread. Luckily she had green thread. It didn't match exactly, but it was passable.

Finishing her project, she eyed the end result, and judged that she did a good job. The dress fit adequately, and was pretty she thought.

Now, it's time to go the bazaar.

CHAPTER 3

CHANGE OF COURSE

Most days she walked at a fast pace, occasionally running the nearly two miles to school. For her, it was an effortless pace. She was a farm girl after all.

The paths through the meadows and forests were well worn from years of children going and coming to school, and from workers traveling between farms. Some days she'd leisurely meander, gazing at the beauty of nature, with all the curiosity of a wide-eyed child.

She especially looked forward to seeing the deer. They always fascinated her, especially when she saw a fawn with its mother. It was captivating.

After that she'd think of her mother, the missed love and affection, and sometimes she'd sob softly.

Today though, there's no chance of tears.

Today, she found herself less interested in the deer, or its fawn, or the birds, or squirrels, or the flowers and trees.

Today, she caught herself skipping along the path with certain zeal.

This had to be the first time in her life that she truly was looking forward to something, to anything. What would this day bring? How much fun would she have? She'd be all alone, on her own with some spare change.

Wearing her mother's dress had her feeling a bit grown up. In a few months, she'd be thirteen, and her mother was married when she was sixteen, only a few years away.

A tune she once heard began to float in her mind and she started humming. She passed the school beaming, and giggled a bit. No school for her today!

As she ascended a small hill, she could hear noise, laughter too. Her skipping increased in speed, and she was more anxious with each step to get to the bazaar which must be over the next hill. Getting closer and closer to the delight that lay ahead was exhilarating. She was now running and realized how much easier this would be if she were wearing her overalls – a distinct advantage to farm clothes.

A dainty dress does hamper.

Quickly reaching the top of the hill, she tripped on a rock, but was able to right herself. As she looked up, she saw it. What a sight! It was so beautiful – The Bazaar. She had no expectations as she had never seen such a sight.

Stopping for a few minutes to catch her breath, and probably her nerve, she walked slowly, head up, towards the gigantic wrought iron gate.

Two distinguished men stood on either side of the gate and their colorful outfits reminded her of the ones she saw in the picture books during the reign of King Henry VIII. It was easy for her to remember that King.

How could he possibly have so many wives? Each guard wore velvety billowy hats with feathers on each side, of varying colors. In their hands they held a metal rod that looked like some kind of spear that was curled on the top end, and that towered above their heads.

Mustering her courage, she approached the gate waiting for the men to stop her from going into the bazaar. To her pleasant surprise, she entered through the gates with ease. They barely noticed her. Once inside, she started to relax.

It was more than she ever could have hoped for. So many things and people to see, games to play, food to eat, and enjoyment at each corner. Would her spare change be enough for the day? She hoped so, and knew she'd have to be prudent.

The bazaar was so loud, almost deafening, and so many things were happening all at once.

Not like the demanded order at home.

Which way to go, which aisle, so many choices! She decided to walk around the bazaar first, before spending her money. This way she could get a good idea as to what she really wanted to spend the meager coinage on.

Most aisles were filled with booths of target games. Hit the target with a fake gun, or arrow, or ball, and win a prize. One booth had a large stuffed dog, and another had a porcelain doll. Oh how she would have loved both.

She watched as sweethearts played winning prizes of all kinds. The losers were not bitter. They simply went to the next booth and tried again. People were shouting, cheering, and the laughter was infectious. She found herself shouting, cheering and laughing which for her, was truly an unusual state.

It felt great! When had she ever felt this way?

The game that especially caught her eye was a mechanical device. It had a mechanized arm picking up all kinds of toys that were displayed on the bottom of the glass enclosed box.

Next, she came across the food aisle — such temptations! These delectables were well beyond her simple meals of porridge, bread, and chicken.

All the sights, sounds, and smells were overwhelming.

One booth's sign read "Photographs" and although she would have loved to have one, she knew it was beyond her means that day.

This booth reminded her of Mr. Handelman, the local tailor who had been fascinated by photography. They had met when she picked up a pair of trousers for Papa.

On that day she entered the shop, and Mr. Handelman came out of the back room explaining he'd been putting away photography equipment.

He saw her face light up.

"Are you interested in photography?" he asked with a cheerful smile.

"I have only seen one photograph and always wondered how they did that!" she explained in an excitable tone.

"Would you like to learn photography?" Mr. Handelman inquired in his kind and gentle manner.

And as she was answering, "Yes, thank you!" he opened the black curtains that separated the front and back of the store and she could see the camera sitting on the bench.

It was that day's occurrence that whetted a thirst for learning – a strong desire to expand her mind. He taught her about daguerreotypes, ambrotypes, and the current tintypes that used japanned iron plates instead of the fragile silver plate, or glass plate surfaces that were previously used.

He promised to take her photograph.

"I will see you soon Mr. Handelman" she exclaimed.

One week later, a sign was posted on the front door explaining that the shop was closed and that Mr. Handelman had died.

As she was remembering that kind gentleman, she became sentimental. She knew that diving into the trunk this morning and wearing this dress, and now reminiscing about Mr. Handelman, brought on this feeling of loss. Today wasn't the day for sentiment and she quickly closed that door.

She started to people watch now. All the ladies were especially well dressed in fine linen or luxurious silk dresses, fashioned for the day. The parasols matched their tiny purses which matched the brimmed sun hats with plumes, both large and small, which further matched every aspect of the ladies' outfit. The colors were gorgeous with rich tones, both deep and vibrant hues, and pastels.

These ladies appeared to be gliding, with such confidence and style.

What elegance and grace!

Walking arm in arm with a gentleman and having his strength to depend on felt so natural to her. Papa never re-married and she wondered if he'd be dependable to a proper lady.

There were many young girls at the bazaar. Some were with their parents or friends, or like her, alone. How wonderful it would be to have one close friend she pondered.

Stopping at a food stand, she ordered a cinnamon bun which was sticky and sweet, and better than anything she'd ever tasted. She licked her fingers with such pleasure. Perhaps she should eat all day! But she knew that wasn't the way to spend the day. So after finishing her delectable, she sauntered back to the main section of the bazaar to play the mechanical machine.

She was drawn to this game in particular because it had gears and pulleys for her to examine. The workings of the machine fascinated her. After intense scrutiny, she inserted her coin into the slot and was able to grab a small stuffed red horse. Could she hold on to it long enough with this mechanical arm and its sharp pointed teeth? It dropped and she was disappointed, but doggedly kept at it.

And yes! She finally held onto the horse long enough to guide it into the opening where she could retrieve it.

As she was retrieving the horse, she noticed a rusty old coin dangling from a string wrapped around the horse's neck. She examined the coin hoping that it had value.

A well-dressed gentleman was standing nearby, and asserted that he could explain the coin. He told her that it was a memento, a trinket, and had no value except its history.

"This is a window into the past. Think of those who have touched this," he said gently.

A warm smile appeared as he helped her remove the coin from around the horse's neck. She put it in her pocket to be placed in her own small treasure chest hidden underneath her bed.

Saying good bye to the kind gentleman, the child played some other games before it was time to leave.

The day went by too fast!

Heading towards the gate, she came across that same gentleman and thanked him again for his help with the coin. As she was turning to face the gate, unexpectedly, the man took hold of her arm.

"May I have the privilege of giving you a ride home? I have a carriage that will whisk you home in no time," he exclaimed with delightful charm and pleasantness.

A carriage, a horse drawn carriage! The child had never been in a carriage and was thrilled at the prospect. Once they exited the gates, the gentleman motioned toward a large black carriage, lavish in its design and comfort, and drawn by two midnight black horses. She'd never seen horses like these before. They were stunning!

An elaborate and ornamental gold embossed letter "H" was on the side of the carriage. Asking what the "H" stood for, the kind gentleman said it was the name of a school and said no more.

The ride didn't take long, and when she reached home, she had a sense of happiness that she'd never felt before

– an amazing feeling.

Cooking dinner tonight wouldn't be the usual chore, for this evening her vivid imagination would play over and over again the wonderful day she experienced.

CHAPTER 4

BEING FIFTEEN

The year is 1879, and Lacey Leighton is turning fifteen next week. She now looks forward to her birthday, being with her friends, and feeling safe. It's too awful for her to bear the thought of what her life would have been like had she not gone to that bazaar.

No longer did she have to worry about her father's anger or temperament. No longer did she have to obey and listen to those absurd brothers of hers – those oafs.

One day she belonged to Papa and his whims, and the next day she was attending The Harlan School for Young Ladies.

She wasn't sure how it happened, and believed the gentleman who gave her the ride home from the bazaar had something to do with it. He came to the house to see Papa, and then she was told she was going to this school. It would prepare her for the life of a young lady. No more overalls, no more chores, no more of Papa's sordid tales.

She's still astounded at the change of circumstance

that led to this day. It all started with the bazaar.

And look where she's at now.

And just look at this dress!

It was hard for her to get used to sleeping and dressing in a dormitory with all the other young girls when she first arrived at Harlan. Now she shares a room with three other girls, and when she's sixteen she will only have one roommate. She's certainly looking forward to that!

The large mirror on the landing allowed her to primp before heading to class. Her long, curly, brunette hair hung down her back, almost to her waist. It was tied with a satin ribbon, and a generous bow was the finishing touch.

Her ivory dress, made of silk taffeta, with its bright cerise lace fit her exquisitely, and was suitable for a young lady her age. Her shoes and corset were uncomfortable, but with patience, she grew to accept them.

Gazing at the reflection in the mirror, she almost didn't recognize herself. Lacey believed she looked different, she felt different. Standing at the top of the landing, she saw a young lady, no longer a child, with manners befitting a blue blood! "Who is that young lady?" she mused, and felt pride in her beauty and etiquette.

She knew the days of wearing overalls with a dirty face and dirty ears were long gone. Now, she looked forward to her future, to her life as a young lady with many prospects and few limitations. She was being educated in the finer things of life and knew her particular intellect and beauty would carry her far, as far as she could go.

She adjusted her ribbon, evened the bow, smoothed down the lace on the bodice, wet her pinky and ran it over her eyebrows, and turned towards the stairs. As she turned, she took one more glimpse at her appearance and smiled a hearty grin.

That reflection confirmed how far she had come.

Instinctively, she held the railing loosely, gliding her hand down the railing as she proceeded gently down the stairs.

Walking down the hallway, she was at peace. Her mind was filled with sweet thoughts, inquisitive thoughts, and yes, a few mundane thoughts too. She oftentimes thought of her teachers, and her mentors.

Her family rarely came to mind.

And the outside world seemed strange and ominous. Being prepared to meet the outside world was why she was here, and it gave her a sense of self, a brass ring – genuine maturity.

A future was now a good thing with endless opportunities and possibilities.

After picking up an extra assignment, she was passing a painting on the wall she especially loved. A year ago she wouldn't have been moved by this art. Now, she can look at it with awe and appreciate its grandeur. Oh, if only she could paint like that.

She had acquired a great deal of confidence since attending Harlan, but confidence in any artistic ability was still lacking. Her mentors tenaciously encouraged her talents and believed that she had special gifts and aptitudes. They knew best, they indicated, and she wanted to believe them. Doubt, regrettably, was pervasive.

And as her instructors had insisted, she began taking singing lessons. Lacey had sung in the church choir when she lived at home and stopped when all she could hear was her father's and brother's criticism.

Singing had proved difficult and she questioned the wisdom of this endeavor. Nonetheless, she kept taking the lessons, kept practicing, and in a short time believed she was actually improving and learning the techniques of singing.

"Do I have talent?" she'd ask herself as a desperate attempt to be convinced that this undertaking wasn't futile. The answer eluded her.

Mr. Young was walking towards her, and as he got closer, Lacey blushed. Did he know of her crush? In class, he always paid extra attention to her. This she knew, and as he passed, he winked, and she felt a rush of heat that startled her.

All the teachers and mentors were so kind, she thought. She had learned so much, and was so grateful to all of them.

Lacey turned the corner and went down another flight of stairs to the second floor. She had never been in a building with so many floors, and she marveled at how such a building could be constructed.

"Such nonsense for a young lady to be thinking about," Mr. Russell had scolded.

A couple of young girls were walking quickly up the same stairs, talking seriously and quietly. Lacey didn't know them well – she knew they were older, probably sixteen. As they passed, they both looked directly at her, saying nothing. Lacey saw something peculiar in their faces. It appeared to her they wanted to say something, but didn't, for whatever reason.

And still, when walking into class, she kept seeing their expressions. They looked pained. Was she imagining this? What could be upsetting them?

Were they trying to tell her something?

Lacey had an inventive imagination and she knew this about herself. Sometimes her imaginings were so intense that reality could not intrude again easily. Not having a mother perhaps added to this propensity, or perhaps created it. Was her imagination causing her to see more than what was really there?

Shaking off this disturbing melancholy, Lacey entered the west wing day room.

CHAPTER 5

ZACHARY

The carriage pulled up in front of *The Harlan School for Young Ladies*. While not an imposing structure – as though purposefully understated – the building's design included a simple but smartly styled façade, and three tall towers topped with steeply pitched and gracefully curved mansard roofs. Two well dressed, well groomed, and handsome young footmen opened the carriage door. Zachary stepped out and onto the steps that led to the entry to the school.

Both footmen opened the main entry doors and one led the young man into a majestic vestibule.

Zachary took a seat as directed and eyed with much satisfaction the grandeur that surrounded him. It was surprising that the inside of the school was in such contrast to the relatively unassuming outside. He was from a wealthy family from New England and was used to stateliness, but the interior beauty of this school was exceptional. Paintings, statues, and marble floors all adorned this vision. What was beyond?

He had turned nineteen last week, and was now expected to grow up and take his position in society and to honor the family's obligations and responsibilities.

Is this how one "grows up?" Zachary pondered. Getting matched with a wife of your father's choosing? It all appeared rather old fashioned.

Zachary was the eldest of his siblings. He wasn't close to his younger brother who had lost or never possessed the ability to reason to good effect. This brother was always getting into trouble for this or for that, and was constantly trying his parent's patience. He didn't want to study at school, nor did he want to play fairly. All this was in direct contrast to Zachary. The only thing they had in common was their looks: medium build, dark thick hair, and deep brown eyes with flecks of gold. They could have been twins, unlike his sister – the youngest of the three, who was fair haired and fair skinned.

She was the one he admired and was close to.

They were each only a year apart yet his brother still acted like a child. His sister, for her young age was most like their mother – a thoughtful and caring woman. This isn't to say that his father wasn't a thoughtful and caring man for he could be at times. But mostly he was gruff and set in his stubborn ways.

Zachary believed that his mother's behavior, which was typically banal, consistently disturbed his father in ways that Zachary couldn't comprehend. He knew that love and marriage wasn't always easy, and decided this tension was the norm for his parents. This was 1880 and the times had changed since the war. To Zachary, his father and his cronies were still living in the stifled age of the Victorian era, but Zachary saw cracks in the walls of those Victorian homes.

Here he sat. He couldn't disobey. Today he'd meet a young lady that his father hoped Zachary would marry within the year.

Absurd!

This was a young man who loved life, and whose principal interest laid in philosophy and science. He was above petty bickering and unkind words and actions.

Father and Zachary had very little in common.

This inquisitive young man was being groomed to take over the family business. It was a lackluster business, and Zachary recoiled at the monotony that lay ahead. But he knew it was his only future and had settled into that reality.

What choice did he have?

Nathaniel Dorsey, Zachary's grandfather, started the company. Prior to that business venture, he'd been a landowner in a small town, and loved the small town life. And, he had been a respected and beloved advisor to many people who lived there. He was known to lease acreage to farmers of low means at an extremely reasonable rent – unheard of in those days.

Dorsey was the sort to give anyone a chance, even a second and third chance. Unfortunately, that consideration had been burned out of him by a gnarly and abusive farrier who took full advantage of him and the town's generosity.

Rumor has it that after that entanglement, Dorsey lost

all faith and trust in his fellow man.

A painful limp had been an unrelenting reminder.

That clash changed Nathaniel Dorsey. His heart and spirit were broken – hard replaced soft, stridence replaced kindness, and love now had to be earned and was in short supply. Seeing this dramatic change in her husband, his wife was unable to offer any consolation.

After selling his lands, he moved with his family to the city, never looking back, and started a business that he could control. It took an open mind to find the right business, and with perseverance he succeeded and became wealthy. He bought the house on the hill typical of someone of his station, and built his legacy. Some years later, there were rumors of financial difficulty, but the company thrived soon after.

His son, Algernon Dorsey, Zachary's father, had turned twenty-four and was vice-president of the company when his father died. Algernon, the only surviving son was anxious to continue his father's legacy.

And he did, rigorously and with cold calculation. Algernon had the fearlessness that his father lacked and was able to turn an unexceptional endeavor into a strong contender in that emerging industrial age.

And that success obviously brought Zachary to this point, to sitting in this school for young ladies, waiting to meet a possible future wife. He was told nothing, except that she was perfect for him.

How would they know?

He was willing to meet the young lady, and perhaps, they'd have things in common, and could talk about things that interested them both.

As he sat there contemplating his future, Zachary thought he heard crying. It stopped as quickly as it began. He reasoned after all that this was a school for young ladies and the sound of crying, well, not that unusual.

His sister cried over the simplest measures.

A gentleman dressed all in black entered the vestibule and requested Zachary to follow him. No introduction, no conversation, no banter.

He followed him through several sets of heavy wooden doors, up the stairs, and down a hall. The walls were filled with paintings and ornate lighting fixtures dangling from the high ceilings. Opulence was bountiful and Zachary wondered why. This was a finishing school for ladies, not a grand castle or home. What tuition must be paid!

Last year, with his parents, Zachary attended a stylish Ball and met the wife of the host, an incredibly fine-looking woman with an appealing name to match – Damaris. She had graduated from The Harlan School many years earlier, and Zachary couldn't help but notice the couples' age difference. The host, a prominent local surgeon, was at least his father's age, and she was perhaps in her early twenties. This was his second marriage.

She smiled politely – not genuinely, he judged.

Her duties were performed perfectly and she was graceful and courteous.

She read a passage from Homer and played the spinet with ease.

Her husband had lost two sons shortly after his first

wife's death, one to disease, and one to foul play. When his child bride bore one son and later a daughter, he was at first distraught. The boy thankfully was healthy, and the father needed to be hopeful.

He watched that child's development vigilantly, hiring the best and most expensive nurses and nursery maids to take complete charge of the child. It was essential that this boy survive in order to be heir to his dynasty.

Zachary knew that this is what his father expected of him. To take over the family business, marry well, and bear children. All else didn't matter.

Love was inconsequential.

Now, at Harlan, he was following the gentleman into a wood paneled room with picture windows that looked out onto a pond. The white feathers of the swans were lit by the brightness of the sun, and the cool blue of the pond mirrored the intense color of the sky. It was an exquisite sight.

There were several young ladies sitting together on settees drinking tea, and across the room were a couple of other young ladies talking with a couple of older gentlemen. Zachary thought that he must be the youngest man in the room, although a couple of the gentlemen may have been a few years older. He reasoned most of these men were thirty to fifty years of age. One seemed older still. And the ladies, well, they were young, younger than he was. Did they truly like talking with the older gentlemen?

A broad-shouldered fellow with a muscular frame introduced himself and on his arm was one of the ladies that had been sitting on the settee. She was petite with small hazel eyes, flaxen hair, and a charming countenance. After introducing Constance, the fellow motioned them to sit in the corner. He brought them freshly brewed mint tea, and warm raisin scones.

Constance reminded Zachary of the wife of his father's friend – the one he met at the Ball last year. It was hard to pinpoint why. But there was a distinct similarity.

While sipping the tea and enjoying the scones, they talked about many things – all of minimal interest to Zachary.

Yet to him, this young lady appeared mechanical in her desire to appeal to him. She sat there with her hands placed perfectly in her lap, not one hair out of place, and a smile, similar to Damaris' that seemed sincere yet at a second glance seemed to be forged.

Was this the young lady his father hoped had an edge over other young ladies Zachary knew? Why this one? What did she have that he needed? And why not introduce him to these other young ladies?

Not wanting to be rude, he politely excused himself and walked into the hall. He walked a bit, and sat down to think about what to tell his father.

Constance wasn't the one.

Would his father accept that?

CHAPTER 6

THE RELIC

Lacey loved these afternoons in the arboretum sitting amid the red maple trees, whose generous foliage offered shade on these warm days.

Under the cloudless azure sky, the tables and chairs rested pristinely. Beautiful bright white toile table cloths with lace embroidery, and fine bone china donned the tables, while a footman served the afternoon tea and the freshly baked basil biscuits. Caramel sweets sat idly on a marble-topped, brass-legged stand waiting to be tasted.

A gentle breeze carried temperate air through the leaves, and the intoxicating fragrance of the Dutch hyacinths wafted in tandem with the serene wind.

There'd be no books, lessons, or singing this afternoon while getting together and resting with her closest friend. She'd known Rueby since her first day at Harlan, and on that day a strong bond grew between them.

Often, Lacey recognized that she received special consideration from the teachers and the mentors. She noticed too that Rueby, and the other girls, didn't get this similar care.

Was there a difference between her and the other girls that promoted such favoritism?

And if so, what was the difference?

Confiding in and telling her friend of these concerns, Rueby would inevitably tell her, "It is only that imagination and curiosity of yours! They will get you in trouble one day."

Lacey would peer at her friend with a smirk, knowing she could be right.

Wanting to read more than vanilla romantic stories, Lacey often snuck into Mr. Young's office and read books on the subjects that fascinated her, especially, science. She wanted to learn and discuss world events. There was so much more than just learning how to dress properly, carrying yourself appropriately, conversing, or commanding servants.

She wanted to fly!

All this inquisitiveness faded as she walked into the arboretum. Lacey sat down and listened to her classmates' stories and offered tales that would be of interest to them.

She'd blend in.

It was always difficult for her to rationalize why they weren't learning what she imagined they should be learning – history and science. The literature they were reading was entertaining but finite. The Arts were filled with beauty but finite too. She knew that young ladies don't grow into world historians, or scientists, but why couldn't they learn a small piece relating to these subjects?

Someday, when she graduated, she'd buy books and learn these things. How excited she'll be – books on shelves, books on tables, books everywhere.

For now, she'll enjoy this adventure.

Lacey walked near the pond to watch the swans. It was a lovely day and the swans were caring for their newborns. She found such joy in watching them.

So free!

After a short time she sat down next to Rueby, and nibbled on the delicious basil biscuits while Rueby sipped the tea.

All the girls were chatting and waiting for Mr. Russell to bring the expected gifts. They each knew that these were special gifts, tokens of their teachers and mentors love.

What would it be today?

Mr. Russell, with his flowing red hair and well-trimmed beard, walked towards them with his familiar jovial smile. He adjusted his vest, his watch and its chain, stood in front of the tables, and prompted the girls to stand and repeat their mission. Each young lady, standing shoulder to shoulder, repeated the statement.

My Harlan mission is:
To be a loyal and obedient young lady;
To be thankful and courteous to all;
To be grateful to my teachers and mentors;
To honor the school; and,
To honor its decisions, without question.

Some had tears in their eyes. The statement was profound. These young ladies loved and respected this school, and their loyalty was resolute. It had given each of them a great opportunity and all they had to do in return was to do as they were told. Most of these girls were either orphans, or from poor families, and their futures were now sealed – sealed for the better and best.

Lucky ladies they were, to be sure.

Weren't they?

After taking their seats, Mr. Russell discussed with the young ladies the meaning of the mission statement, and how pleased the school was with each and every one of them.

"And, as a gesture of the school's affection, we are handing out a gift that we hope you will each cherish," he announced with an air of awe and wonderment.

"They are relics, antique coins," he clarified. "Each is of great value and should be kept in a safe place. They were discovered recently on an old ship wreck that sunk in the ocean nearly one hundred years ago, and the school bought them specifically for their young ladies. Nothing is too good for Harlan young ladies!

These coins are windows into the past.

Think of those who have touched these."

After finishing his talk, and as the presents were being handed out, Mr. Russell stood there for a few moments observing the innocent faces of his young charges. He watched as the young ladies opened their gifts with great anticipation, while Lacey was last to open hers.

Mr. Russell's last two sentences startled Lacey. They

were the same words the older gentlemen said to her about the bazaar trinket. This coincidence put her on edge.

She opened her gift, now with fervor, and as she eyed the present, her heart thumped. She stared at the relic, the antique coin – the trinket! This was the same coin she won at the bazaar, wasn't it? The trinket from the bazaar was in her room, in her secret sachet, along with mementos.

But how could this be? She must be wrong. As she was examining it, her pulse raced, and after asking Mr. Russell to be excused, went directly to her room.

At first she walked down the hall at the standard pace befitting a young lady at Harlan, and then, quite unexpectedly, her step quickened. She ran up the stairs, down another hall, and was trembling when her hand touched the door knob to her room. Pausing, she caught her breath and stood straight, turned the knob, and opened the door.

Her reaction to the gift was unsettling. What was so disturbing? She grinned slightly at her overreaction and nodded her head somewhat. At this point, she just wanted to compare the two coins. Surely they weren't the same – they couldn't be.

The secret sachet was in her bottom drawer, underneath petticoats. She took each petticoat out of the drawer, neatly laying them on the bed. Next, reaching into the drawer she retrieved the sachet, and realized she was trembling.

"This could *not* be the same coin," she said out loud.

The bazaar coin was worthless, a Carney prize, not an antique or relic, and certainly not from a lost ship recently found.

If it is the same coin, what does this mean?

Mr. Russell's words crept back into her mind:

"These are windows into the past.
Think of those who have touched these."

Lacey reproached herself once more for being irrational. Coincidences occur frequently!

Abruptly, she closed the top of the secret sachet without examining her trinket, and put the sachet back into the drawer placing her neatly folded petticoats quickly back in their place. "They cannot be the same! All I need to do is to compare them. What is stopping me from doing that?" she chided herself in a quiet whisper.

"If they *are* the same, it could only mean that the school is lying to us."

But why would they lie, what do they have to gain? They're our mentors, our heroes, she silently contemplated.

Or: could the mentors have been deceived?

She had her doubts as to that alternative.

As she was putting the sachet back in its secret place, her heart thumped again. She stood there for several minutes, staring. Instinctively, now with no reluctance, she pulled out, once more, all her petticoats from the drawer, flinging them on the bed aimlessly and reached for the sachet.

Now, grasping the sachet, she sat back down, and slowly, gently opened it. First she took out the small red pony and held it tightly. Then, she hesitantly reached deeper into the sachet, moving objects out of the way until she found the coin. It was wrapped in a bright scarlet satin ribbon that was her mother's. Slowly she separated the ribbon from the coin.

Lacey looked intensely at it.

Her eyes were fixated and it took a minute before she could look away. She had laid Mr. Russell's coin on the stand next to the bed, and now she leaned over and picked it up with her free hand.

Back and forth her eyes darted between the two coins, examining and comparing every nuance, every bit of rust, every indention, and raised letter.

There could be no doubt. These two coins were the same. One was removed from a toy at a bazaar and was valueless. The other, given by Mr. Russell today, had great worth, so they were told.

Was it merely a mistake or misunderstanding?

Or, was this a deliberate lie, deception?

Lacey sat there for several minutes weighing the various likelihoods. Without forethought, she stood up abruptly and surveyed the room as if seeing it for the first time, as if in an introspective trance.

Several minutes later, her mind took sharp focus, and she imagined a scheme, a scheme to control – a scheme *to produce a certain type of young lady*: one that does not question the mission statement!

But to what end?

Lacey shuddered.

If they lied about this inconsequential gift, what else have they lied about?

Another shudder took hold.

Composing herself as best she could, she sat back down as an unexpected giggle broke the silence, and a tiny smirk swept across her face.

Was this strange affair strictly the imaginings of an anxious mind? Why a scheme?

Perhaps the treasure was found recently, and recently could be a few years ago. Perhaps the coin from the bazaar has substantial value too? It's possible.

Lacey, after careful consideration, did not believe either of these scenarios, and continued to sit on the bed still needing to allay her fear. Was she simply being childish? She hadn't felt trepidation since coming to Harlan, yet now she wondered if there was something untoward about the school.

Untoward! Why was she thinking that?

Then unexpectedly, she remembered something important —the *shadow*. She sees it now and then and did tell Mr. Russell about it last year. He said it must be the maids or the footman working hard, trying not to disturb, and to put it out of her mind. Is this connected to this day's fear?

She closed her eyes and forced herself to sing a ditty she had learned the other day. It helped her calm down.

A knock at the door broke her focus.

"Are you alright Lacey?" her mentor inquired.

"I will be right there, Mr. Russell," Lacey explained.

She quickly put her trinket back in the sachet and buried it under the petticoats, closed the drawer, then opened the door.

Telling him that she had felt a little faint and just needed to lie down, she closed the door behind her assuring him that she was feeling much better and walked with him back to the arboretum.

"How do you like your gift Lacey," he queried.

"It is a part of history – I love it," she declared with feigned fascination.

CHAPTER 7

A CHANCE MEETING

Zachary couldn't fathom why his father was so insistent that Constance was "the one." Why not introduce him to all the girls and let providence take hold. Walking around the halls of this finishing school only brought on more questions.

His sister was at a finishing school and it wasn't like this!

Philadelphia is a nice place, he supposed, if you like the city life, though this school is many miles outside the city. He didn't care for city life. He much preferred the country and the slow and quiet pace that was the preference of those that lived there.

And especially, is there not a notable difference between New England sensibility and Philadelphia's insatiable character?

His father, apparently, preferred long periods in the city to the serenity of the country. Nonetheless, he bought the country estate and moved his family there. He visited home when there was a Gala or a birthday, and never stayed long, which was obviously painful for his wife.

Knowing his father's business, and that it was conducted in the city always brought on consternation for Zachary. He had hoped to attend Harvard, or Yale, allowing him many years before taking on business responsibility.

That wasn't the plan. "His son," the father proclaimed, would receive education through business endeavors – real world experience vs. stodgy educators.

Zachary much preferred to be a physician or a scholar, studying history and science. He knew that these natural inclinations served no purpose to the father. There was no question that the son was required to take on the business that had been built across these many years.

For the son, there seemed to be no way out.

Today, he was here, in this school, looking for a wife, of all things. Constance was nice enough and they did have some things in common.

He spoke French, and so did she.

He loved horses, and so did she.

He preferred Beethoven, and so did she.

He didn't care for Mozart, and neither did she.

Dancing, he explained, was never his forte, and she confessed, she preferred to watch.

He disliked large social gatherings, and yes, Constance felt the same.

At first, he was suspicious of their commonalities, and he tested her the best way he knew how, but in the end, he believed she meant what she said. In spite of that, she wasn't the one. He knew this in his heart. Nothing could change his mind.

Thinking of this only made matters worse. Was he expecting too much? What was he looking for? On the surface, Constance was an uncannily perfect match.

It was as if she was made for him!

Not knowing how much time had passed since he left Constance for a seat in the hall, Zachary became concerned that he may be considered rude for leaving her. He needed a breather – more time to contemplate his father's deed.

Zachary spotted an arched walkway that led outside, opening to a manicured garden that beckoned him. The flowers were either in bloom or about to bloom, and the scents and the colors were overpowering. Tall, thick hedges formed a small maze on the west side of the garden, while handsome trees lined the pathways. He recognized rose bushes and irises; other flowers were new to him.

Sitting down on a white stone bench that sat underneath an old willow tree, he closed his eyes and felt the warmth of the summer heat, and let the fragrances surround him.

Hearing footsteps he knew instantly they were coming for him. Standing up, he walked towards them and quickly decided on an excuse as to why he had stayed away so long. A young lady came out of a pathway and nodded as she passed. Zachary ventured that she was the most beautiful girl he had ever seen, and when their eyes met, he felt his heart skip a beat.

She glided by, with such grace. He knew what he was feeling was fantasy. He didn't know her, yet her eyes had such tenderness, gentleness. And the warmth of her smile when she passed was so genuine and sincere.

She had walked a few paces past Zachary when he stood up and introduced himself.

"My name is Zachary Dorsey and I am visiting Harlan for a few days. May I ask your name, and would you consider walking in the garden with me?"

Lacey blushed, and replied in a quiet whisper, "I am Lacey Leighton, and I would be happy to walk with you." The name Leighton seemed familiar somehow, but he didn't know why. He had heard it before. Was it that common of a name?

"Your last name seems familiar to me. Do you have relatives in New England?" Zachary inquired.

"My parents are deceased," she responded immediately, "and I do not have any other living relatives."

Zachary was pained by her admission. He could live without his father, and brother, but he loved his mother and sister greatly and couldn't imagine a world without them.

A few moments later, Lacey headed towards the door that led inside.

"Do you have a moment or two to sit in the garden with me a while longer?" he inquired.

It was after all the sweet of summer days.

Lacey stood there holding Mr. Russell's coin in her hand. What was the truth behind the two coins? She chose to keep hope that the coin incident was probably nothing at all, or purely a misunderstanding. Wanting to put this confusion to rest, she quickly put the coin in her velvet purse, and thought sitting with a young man in this humbling garden would be good for her at this precise moment.

"Yes, shall we sit down?" Lacey said pointing to a wooden bench that sat next to an immense oak tree with red roses in bloom on all sides.

Zachary took off his coat and laid it down on the bench for her to sit on. What kindness. They both sat down with reasonable distance between them. Lacey opened her parasol and glanced ardently at the roses.

Silence, and more silence. Neither spoke for quite a while.

Breaking the awkward silence, Zachary informed Lacey that he was here visiting at his father's request and further explained how impressed he was with this school, its beauty, and its surroundings. He solicited many questions, and she answered honestly. She found it easy to talk with him and was thankful she had met him this afternoon.

"He must have read my mind," she thought as she heard him say the same.

A bell was ringing in the distance, and Lacey had to leave. It was the dinner bell, and she needed time to change.

"When can I see you again?" Zachary requested.

"We do not date gentlemen until we are sixteen," she expressed amiably.

He was undaunted.

"Nonsense! You are almost sixteen, and we are only getting to know each other. How can that be wrong?"

Lacey agreed.

CHAPTER 8

THE SOIREE

They agreed to meet that night in the garden. If the evening's adventure went well, tomorrow, Lacey, of course would get permission from Mr. Russell to see this young man again.

After dinner was finished, she hurried to her room to re-dress for the anticipated evening. She was in a state of nervous excitement and could hardly breathe.

She had a choice of several dresses to wear that evening and as she was deciding on which one to wear, she suddenly stepped back. An old memory came to mind – picking out a dress from her mother's keepsake chest – and she shook her head in amazement. That memory and those days were long gone. And now she stood here, having to decide which of several exquisite dresses to wear.

Amazing!

She chose the celadon dress with its crimson lace and full bustle – the latest fashion. This silhouette certainly showed off her hourglass figure which appeared last year.

The ruler is gone.

Now she's beyond any doubt, a woman.

Just look at her!

A woman off to see a young man!

Lacey was finally flying.

As she was tying the ribbon around her hair, she wondered why Zachary was here. Since his father had sent him to Harlan, most likely he was here for the soirees. She wondered how she'd compare to all the young ladies he'd meet during his visit.

She knew that when the girls reached sixteen there was an afternoon soiree with gentlemen of all ages, from all parts of the world. This gathering offered a relaxing venue for the gentlemen to meet Harlan's young ladies.

The visitors would stay for several days attending several soirees, a gala, riding horses, and walking in the gardens. Lacey noticed that after that, these men convened with the various mentors of the school.

She assumed that these days enabled the girls to gain experience with gentlemen suitors, and perhaps to learn the finer points of courtship. And further, these get-togethers allowed the young ladies to broaden their proficiencies.

It was the path to maturity.

During the next year, these gentlemen would visit the school. They watched as the young ladies blossomed and grew to appreciate their societal responsibilities. They were becoming proficient in various skills such as foreign language, the arts, and perhaps playing the spinet or the muselar. Their appearance and their gait were developing;

even their voices appeared sweeter.

They would have been guided and instructed by their teachers and mentors as to which skill was best suited for them. It was obvious that the young ladies were unable to search their own soul for their own special talent.

No, the teachers and mentors had the ability, not them.

Until the young ladies reached, with only a few exceptions, their seventeenth birthday, these same men visited with varying routines. A young lady might meet individually with a particular visitor, and she'd show him what she had learned.

One young lady might read The Iliad with emotion and appreciation, while another might read the same classic with stoicism. Another could be reciting Edgar Allan Poe, or singing. Or, possibly, the young lady would converse in the gentleman's native language.

And still another may demonstrate her proficiency on not just one in the family of harpsichords, but all three. A Virginals harpsichord was in the Dining Room, a Muselar harpsichord was in the West Parlor, and a Spinet harpsichord was in the Ball Room. The school also had a fortepiano in the classroom and it was taught as well as the harpsichord.

The music teacher, Mr. Keane, preferred the harpsichord to the fortepiano. He felt the harpsichord sounded exactly as the angels should sound and the fortepiano was exactly as human's do sound.

On that seventeenth birthday, these young women graduated.

Lately, Lacey had been conflicted with the woman's role in society. The Harlan girls, including Rueby, wanted to be married, have children, and run a home.

What was the alternative – to be a spinster and to live a lonely existence?

This didn't seem right to Lacey. These ladies, these spinsters, did have choices didn't they? Couldn't they have done more with their lives? This was the beginning of the 1880's and the woman's suffragette movement was allowing dreams to become a reality.

Women now have choices!

Meeting the right gentlemen, Lacey theorized, could change her mind, and she'd be the dutiful wife with only slight reservation.

Would she ever meet this special fellow? Was Zachary the one?

If not, and she doesn't meet her special gentleman at Harlan, she'd rather be on her own after graduation. A loveless marriage wasn't a consideration.

Her dreams were not impossible dreams for a young lady, she trusted. And, if she wasn't getting married soon after graduation, she'd immediately embark on her own quest.

As she was putting on her earrings and matching bracelet her mind caught a glimpse of a haunting memory. An old man was watching her. She first noticed it a few weeks before the bazaar. He never approached her and always stayed in the shadows. She'd look away for no more than a second, and he'd be gone.

Could it be her imagination? Thinking this gave her

shivers and she didn't know why. Yet, the memory persisted. So why think of it now?

She shook off the dismal feeling by remembering Zachary, and a flush of warmth came over her. Her cheeks were red and hot and she smiled widely and laughed quietly. Catching her composure, she turned and left her bedroom.

Walking quickly, Lacey went through the double doors that led to the stairs, and stopped unexpectedly at the landing. Backing up, she turned to face the mirror. Could this be the same young lady that was here yesterday scrutinizing this same reflection?

Another striking change had occurred.

*　*　*　*　*　*

Zachary was running late. Another soiree had been organized and he found it difficult to excuse himself. He kept looking at his pocket watch and the hands were moving too slowly. He was worried that this get together could run too long and he'd miss meeting Lacey.

They had arranged a time that hopefully allowed for overruns like this, but he was becoming anxious. His foot was tapping too fast, and he kept looking at his watch too often.

Finally, one gentleman rose out of his seat gleefully announcing that this had been a lovely evening and it was getting late, and shall we call it a night. Zachary politely kissed Constance's hand and bid her farewell and a good night. She looked up at him with fondness and trust, and said she'd see him tomorrow.

Ambling back to her room, Constance reminisced

about the sweet young man she was getting to know.

Zachary's walk, in contrast, was fast and deliberate as he headed towards the garden.

Lacey was sitting on the same wooden bench that she and her new gentlemen friend were sitting on earlier that day. Now Zachary was late. Had he been delayed, or, did he change his mind?

The soiree was a showcase, she knew this. And, judging that its real purpose was strictly a lesson that offered experience in meeting gentlemen, Lacey presumed that it could lead to future relationships.

Just then, Zachary came down the pathway and stood and gazed at Lacey for a second or two.

"May I sit next to you," he asked politely. Lacey enthusiastically replied "yes, of course."

It was getting dark and they'd been talking for hours. Both Zachary and Lacey kept the conversation going. There was so much to say, to ask, to learn, and to plan.

He explained that his father had sent him to get to know Constance, his future wife, and for better or worse, he wasn't interested in her that way. Lacey explained that she believed the soirees were lessons that offered a comfortable and safe environment to learn how to act and what to expect when with a gentleman – a positive encounter.

They both stared at each other in disbelief. Their perceptions were polar opposites.

Zachary explained further that he was sworn to secrecy as to why he was here – a dubious condition. Lacey couldn't understand how this could be so confusing. It had always been simple: a lesson in social surroundings. She knew too that some of the girls became infatuated with some of the gentlemen callers, but that was their mistake, they could get hurt.

Standing up and pacing, Zachary disclosed that he didn't care as to the true reason for the soiree. All he knew was that he cared greatly for Lacey. She blushed and told him the same. They talked late into the night, until the grounds keeper was locking the doors. Each hurried inside and took a moment to hold hands. Zachary gently squeezed Lacey's hands together as he placed a loving kiss on them. A tear streamed down her face.

She had never been this joyful, this tranquil.

This was true happiness.

Zachary only had one more day and one more night before he was leaving. Lacey wanted to tell Mr. Russell about their friendship; she didn't want any impropriety. They parted with anticipation and looked forward to seeing each other tomorrow.

Love was in bloom.

CHAPTER 9

LIGHT OF DAY

Lacey never slept well and getting out of bed was always difficult. Those fitful nights didn't stop even after coming to Harlan. Yet today, thinking of Zachary helped propel her out of bed.

After the chambermaid filled the ewer with water and left the room, Lacey washed up, and was glowing in anticipation of the day that lay ahead. The ladies maid stood at attention waiting for Lacey to need her assistance getting dressed and styling her hair.

Opening the curtains offered primrose sunshine, and the sky was the color of a robin's egg. Her mood couldn't be better.

Lacey flew out the door and down the hall, and practically knocked Rueby off her feet. Rueby stared at her in disbelief.

"This is not how a Harlan young lady strolls down the hall Lacey!" she alleged seriously while trying to hold back a wink and a mischievous grin.

Lacey was surprised at her own eagerness this morning

and wanted to tell Rueby all about Zachary, but she needed to see Mr. Russell before breakfast. Apologizing and hugging her best friend with a promise to tell her everything, she bounded off once again. Rueby watched Lacey flit down the hall and through the doors leading to the stairs; she simply shook her head as she wondered what great journey Lacey was enjoying.

Mr. Russell was planning his agenda for that day when Lacey Leighton walked into his office just before breakfast. He was surprised to see her, here, in his office, this time of day.

"Come in Lacey and have a seat," he instructed in a gentle tone.

He was sitting at his large oak desk and she sat in one of the two overstuffed velvet chairs opposite him. This was a masculine room, indeed, with dark rugs, dark walls, and a large fireplace with a dead animal's head looming above it. Lacey never understood hunting. She hated and loathed it. Having to kill the farm animals to eat was hard enough, but killing for no reason except a sadistic thrill went against Lacey's core. It was barbaric.

Today, as usual, she had to ignore the barbarism and inform Mr. Russell as to her previous day and evening with Zachary. She told him of their chance meeting, how they talked for hours, and that they wanted to see each other again.

The encounter could help her grow, and would provide a chance to converse on a variety of subjects.

Mr. Russell seemed to be listening to her words.

Mr. Russell seemed to grasp the situation, and he

seemed to agree with her.

Lacey relaxed a bit as it was obvious that he couldn't have any objection to this new friendship.

"I will see what I can do as to this young man. Perhaps you two can meet later in the day. Come back by my office early this afternoon," her mentor voiced in a candid style.

Lacey stood up, thanked him, and headed towards the door.

"He must be a special young man, Lacey," he added quickly.

Turning around to face Mr. Russell, Lacey responded "Yes I think he is."

* * * * * *

Breakfast for the teachers and mentors was finished and Mr. Russell hurriedly strode to Mr. Olson's office, the head school master. He closed the door. A letter was written to Zachary's father, to be sent directly, and was handed to the footman with written instructions attached. Mr. Russell ordered the same footman to bring Zachary Dorsey to his office immediately. The footman walked to the wing where the gentlemen guests were housed, and who were now finishing breakfast.

He spotted his quarry, walked to him and politely requested that he follow him. Zachary expected the request to be about Lacey, and was thrilled at the prospect of seeing her again. Zachary sailed into Mr. Russell's office.

Pointing to the same chair that Lacey had occupied earlier, Mr. Russell demanded that the young man sit down. Zachary walked around the large chair, sat down, and noticed a stern face scrutinizing him from across the desk. Now, he felt uneasy. He didn't exactly expect a fanfare, but this formidable look took him by surprise.

A lecture began by addressing the mission of the school, its history, its members, and the importance of following the rules – the ones that keep this dream alive. Zachary had no idea what Mr. Russell was talking about. What members? What rules? What does a finishing school have to do with all of this? The more he heard, the more alarmed he became.

"Your father sent you here for one purpose: to meet Constance, your future wife, and not to indulge in impractical or useless situations. Constance has been groomed and tailored for you. She will run your household, make all preparations necessary for social engagements, and be the mother of your children.

She will *not* question your private life!

She *is* the perfect wife for you."

Mr. Russell's words stung with each syllable, and Zachary was beginning to comprehend the truth behind the school.

A biting coldness crept down the ridge of his spine.

One of the footmen entered Mr. Russell's office holding two suitcases that Zachary immediately recognized.

"What is he doing with my suitcases," he queried with a distressed pitch.

"You are leaving Harlan, and leaving right now. Your belongings have been packed!" Mr. Russell emphatically barked.

And as those words hung in the air, a sizeable footman came in and took Zachary strongly by the arm and escorted him down the hall, down the stairs, out the front door, and into the waiting carriage.

* * * * * *

It was passed lunch time, and shortly she'd see Zachary and they would discuss all sorts of things. Yesterday they talked about their personal lives and their disappointments. Last evening, they talked about philosophy, and the stars above – something called astronomy. And while in bed last night, her head swelled with all the new information and ideas that sparked her inquisitiveness.

Lacey felt so alive.

She had been summoned, and as she entered Mr. Russell's office, she could hardly contain her excitement. When and where would she meet Zachary? She sat down in the same chair she had occupied previously that morning, and waited for Mr. Russell to look up from the papers he was grading.

Putting down papers and his gold pen, he leaned forward, and said with a hint of satisfaction, "Good news Lacey. Your young man will meet you in the garden at two o'clock this afternoon. And after dinner, you may meet again."

Lacey was so pleased and appreciative that she was unable to bring forth a "thank you." Instead, she nodded heartedly, stood up, quickly walked to the door, turned to face Mr. Russell, and uttered "thank you," softly and quietly.

Two o'clock was now an hour away and Lacey wanted to look her best. Rueby tied Lacey's hair ribbon tightly so there'd be no loose hair strands. At first, Ruby wasn't entirely convinced that Lacey's adventure was a good one. Who was this Zachary? After further conversation, Rueby put aside her misgivings.

They both stood there, staring at the reflection in the mirror in Lacey's room, and for all their maturity snickered like children. Rueby wanted to see and hear what was to take place between Lacey and this young gentleman. It was unfair that she'd be left out of the afternoon's fun. But she knew that this was Lacey's day, Lacey's big adventure, and it wasn't to be spoiled by an overzealous supporter. Rueby bid Lacey adieu.

It was now a few minutes before two o'clock and Lacey opened the door to her room and walked into the hall. The world looked different – brighter, less daunting. She had already forgotten the oddities that had haunted her: peculiar looks, shadowy figures, relics. Elation and satisfaction ruled the day. In a few minutes she'd be with Zachary and their journey together would begin. He'd visit her here, and perhaps she'd be able to visit New England and his home.

The possibilities were endless and her mind was examining all of them.

Resting on the same wooden bench they both had sat on the previous evening, she recalled their conversation, and marveled at the enjoyment today would bring.

It was time to look at her watch again. She'd already

looked at it several times.

This watch had been given to her by one of the mentors and she wore it on her bodice with pride. But now she wondered if the watch was running fast. It read two-thirty and Zachary hadn't come. She didn't mind his being late a few minutes but this was too long.

Standing up, Lacey walked inside and caught a glimpse of the tall Grandfather clock that stood next to the archway leading to the garden. Its ornate brass hands pointed to the two and the six: it was two-thirty.

Lacey was anxious. Did he get the message? She'd been told that the note was sent. Yet, he wasn't here.

At two-forty she left the garden and hurried to Mr. Russell's office.

"Come in," he said hearing a knock at the door. There he was at his desk still grading papers.

Standing in front of the desk and contemplating what to say, Lacey stood there, expressionless.

"Sit down Lacey," he said, but she chose to stand.

After a few minutes of stillness, she asked if it was possible that Zachary didn't receive the note.

"I have been in the garden since two o'clock and he has not shown up," she explained with a tense declaration.

Mr. Russell let her chatter about her disappointment, and again invited her to take a seat. She followed his request, and sat down.

There was a difference in her mentor's voice, his tone, and Lacey immediately stiffened.

"Has something happened to Zachary? Has he fallen

ill?"

Mr. Russell gazed at Lacey, cleared his throat, and said he needed to be honest.

"Do you not want me to be honest Lacey?" he prodded. To this she could only nod.

"I know he got the note because I delivered it myself." Mr. Russell continued.

"He was not interested. In fact, a little before lunch, he boarded a carriage and headed to the station to board a train for home."

Lacey could feel her blood drain. Her heart was beating too fast, and she was beginning to feel dizzy.

"It cannot be," she said with sincere reservation.

Mr. Russell offered her a glass of water and as she sipped it she could only see Zachary's face. Had she only imagined their bond and their feelings for each other?

She must have.

Were the feelings only on her side?

Zachary was gone, and with that, he took her heart.▢

CHAPTER 10

THE TRUTH

He was numb.

It was impossible to reason out this day. Their reaction to a friendship at that school was unreasonable and incomprehensible. Wait until he tells Father!

The rocking motion of the Pennsy helped Zachary disentangle from the events that occurred over the past few days, as well as affording the time to muster the words of damnation for that school. What were they running? His father will be appalled.

And, what is the true story encircling Constance?

He arrived home shortly after dinner, following his trip on the Pennsylvania Railroad and a three-day stagecoach journey. He found that his father wasn't home. After greeting his mother, brother, and sister, Zachary went to his bedroom to lie down.

The Housekeeper knocked on the door asking if she could come in and unpack his things. She was a plump older woman with thinning gray hair that always pinned in a tight bun on the top of her head. Zachary and the Housekeeper had developed a strong bond over her many years of service to his family. As she explained that his valet had gone on an errand, Zachary inquired as to when his father was returning.

"He should be home soon," she said gently.

His sister came into his room shortly after the Housekeeper had finished unpacking. Though he was gone barely ten days, his sister had missed him terribly.

"It is not the same when you are gone," she revealed with loving sincerity.

"Mother and Father get along better when you are here. I do not know why, but they do. Perhaps you act as some sort of buffer!" she mused.

There was certainty in her voice.

It was prudent to tell his sister only part of the story regarding The Harlan School. His mother had also questioned him about his visit, and he purposely said very little. Zachary didn't understand the full picture that surrounded the school. He only knew there was a story to be told.

The school's insistence that he spend his time with Constance and no one else was uncivil, both to her and to him. Had she been trained to be his wife? If this is true, and he refuses her, what becomes of her? Re-train her for someone else? More questions than answers.

It was now dark, with no signs of Father. Zachary went to the kitchen to grab a bite to eat and went back to his room. He always held that it was pompous to pull the cord, wait for a servant, and ask them to get him a snack from the kitchen. Why not simply get it yourself, even if it did seem to put the kitchen staff off their mettle.

These tiny acts of defiance always ruffled his father's feathers, and Zachary always relished those occasions.

After eating, he undressed, got into bed and fell asleep immediately. He dreamt of Lacey and The Harlan School, and the dream immediately turned into a nightmare.

Lacey was standing at the top of a hill, all alone, looking down onto a vast valley. The wind was blowing and gun shots could be heard in the distance. Lacey would duck behind a fallen branch that offered little protection from any flying bullets. Then a dark figure came into view and laughed with a hideous intonation. He was carrying a staff that appeared to be made of various kinds of creatures that hissed and curled in all directions. Suddenly, a large bird with a vast wing span flew over Lacey and its talons grabbed hold of the back of her dress. Clutching the dress tightly, the bird flew high into the sky, and as suddenly as the bird appeared, it just as suddenly released her and she fell back to earth.

Zachary awoke drenched in sweat, and was fitful the rest of the night. He couldn't remember ever having such a graphic, horrifying dream. A couple of hours before dawn, sleep finally took hold.

The sun brought Zachary out of his sleep as its rays streamed into the bedroom. Lying in bed half awake, Zachary considered how much the valet does for him, such as the simplest of things, like opening and closing curtains.

The bedroom door opened and in walked the valet full of cheer.

"Good Morning," the valet chimed.

"We have missed your presence. I hope your trip was enjoyable," he added.

Zachary always liked his valet, but this morning he found the valet's cheer irritating.

"Good to see you too Walter," he said with as much graciousness as he could rally.

He watched Walter tidy up, then pick out his clothes for the day.

Choosing the gold studs with the tiny emeralds and matching cuff links, Walter placed the items on the dresser. He waited for Zachary to wash and helped him get dressed. Walter eased the studs and cuff links into place, and took a small brush to the jacket removing any lint.

"Are these not a bit fancy for daytime?" Zachary asked.

Walter explained that his coming home is a special circumstance and that a grand lunch has been prepared.

Moreover, guests arrived late last night and will be joining the family for the lunch. Breakfast trays had been prepared and sent to their rooms.

Guests! A grand lunch! Suspicion was ruling.

Zachary passed his mother's bedroom on his way to the stairs, and heard her arguing with her husband. He couldn't clearly identify what they were saying, but he was certain that his father's words were unsympathetic. His father often spoke harshly to his wife, and she usually stayed silent. Yet here she was arguing with him, voicing whatever opinion she was impressing upon him.

At that moment, the son felt immense respect for his mother. He questioned what could have been so important as to take on her husband. It was rare, it wasn't done.

Not wanting to confront his father immediately after his parent's altercation, Zachary went back to his bedroom.

After a few minutes, he could hear his father's hardened footsteps coming down the hall, and marching down the marble stairs. Soon after, Zachary walked down the same hall, down the same marble stairs, and into the dining room for breakfast. A few minutes later the rest of the family sauntered in, taking their prospective seats.

The conversation at the breakfast table was strained and Zachary observed that his father was impatient and on edge.

"I am glad to see you are home and well," his father declared with a terse timbre.

Nodding his head, Zachary expressed how good it was

to be home, and that he wanted to speak with him at his earliest allowance regarding his trip.

"We have plenty of time for that, and more importantly, I expect you here for lunch," his father declared with no room for disagreement.

Zachary simply nodded.

* * * * * *

It was now noon and lunch would be at one o'clock. Zachary's sister reported that two guests were joining them for lunch. She was surprised because it was such short notice, and furthermore, she didn't know who the guests were. It was a mystery. Zachary explained that Walter had told him the same thing.

Precisely at one o'clock, two guests were escorted into the dining room before the family came in. They both sat as instructed and sipped the refreshment given to them.

The slender older gentlemen sitting at the table had to be at least six feet tall, with large gray eyes and a handlebar mustache that was impeccable. The young lady wore a stylish and chic dress with her hair pulled back in a fashionable loose bun which accented her small but appealing hazel eyes. They said nothing to each other and waited for the family.

The first family member to arrive in the dining room was Father. He thanked his guests for coming and assured them both that all would be worked out. The young lady looked confused.

Mother arrived next, followed by Zachary's sister and brother. Zachary entered the dining room last.

As he entered, he caught a glimpse of Constance. Why

was she here? He took his seat and was fidgeting with dismay and apprehension as to the true purpose of the lunch. The gentleman sitting next to him wasn't at all familiar – who was he?

The first course was served, and the conversation was ordinary. Father asked his guests how their trip was, and inquired as to whether or not the young lady had ever been to this part of the country.

Zachary's sister and brother asked polite questions and the responses were minimal at best. His mother was attentive to the conversations, but did not speak. When dessert was served, Zachary was exceedingly distrustful of this rendezvous.

What were they up to?

"Mother, please show Constance around the estate while we talk business," Father conveyed with a flavor of sweetness not at all typical of him.

Mother replied politely and along with her daughter, directed Constance through the dining room door into the great hall. She'd show her the grandeur of their house, the grounds and the stables. Zachary's brother had already left on his own to go hunting.

After Mother left the dining room, Father directed the older gentleman and Zachary into the library, across the hall. Each took a seat facing each other, and all was silent.

Father re-introduced the older gentleman. At lunch Zachary had been so distracted that he didn't catch the gentlemen's name. His mind was strictly on Constance.

"Zachary, this is Harlan Leighton. He knew your grandfather well. In fact your grandfather was a major contributor to The Harlan School for Young Ladies before you were born. It is what allowed your grandfather and our family to expand our business free of debt."

Zachary glowered. Leighton? Was he related to Lacey? His apprehension continued to grow.

The older gentleman, this Harlan Leighton, rose to his feet and lectured directly to Zachary, with a tempestuous attitude.

"The school provides decent and moral young ladies to decent and moral gentlemen from all walks of life in order for them to succeed in this uneasy world. It is a great service we are providing and the young ladies are given all the best that life can offer. Years of hard work and great care are utilized in order to match each man with the proper lady – the perfect wife."

As the last of these disdainful words were disgorging from Harlan Leighton's lips, he walked towards Zachary and put his formidable hands on his shoulders and squeezed.

Exceedingly clear to Zachary was the exact intention of this school – to provide wives bred in manners and interests suited to the husband, wives of submission and servitude.

Did the young ladies have any say as to whether or not they wanted to marry the chosen spouse? And he answered himself immediately: not likely.

He grasped why he was sitting there. Constance had been primed for him and perhaps bought for him. The idea made him sick to his stomach.

The two older gentlemen curtly justified their mission.

Zachary was going to marry Constance in the next few months. She'd visit and get to know Zachary and the family here, not at the school. When challenged why not at the school, Mr. Leighton said that at this point it was good for Constance to see her new home, and to learn the responsibilities that go with it. A plausible response, but Zachary knew it was because of Lacey.

"You will marry Constance! A lot of preparation and money has been spent on her and you will not refuse." Father spewed.

"I ordered her specifically for you, with your likes and dislikes always in mind – your needs, your desires. How could you not be satisfied with her?" Father added.

Zachary was appalled at the idea that he should marry someone he didn't love.

This took his mind back to Lacey. He wanted to know of any possible relationship between Lacey Leighton and Harlan Leighton, but something deep within him stopped any inquiry. Feeling that this was dangerous territory, he squelched his inquisitiveness. All banter needed to be confined strictly to the matter at hand – Constance.

He wouldn't mention Lacey Leighton.

As he continued to defend his position against marrying Constance, both men shook their heads in rhythm and instructed Zachary, with no hesitation, that his choices were limited. He didn't want her to suffer the obvious consequence, did he?

Obvious consequence!

Zachary had a sickening sense as to what that meant. And, before he could ask anything further, his father leaned towards him and said shamelessly and stingily, "elimination."

That word *elimination* hung frostily in the air, and Zachary was motionless, unable to react quickly to the meaning of the word. After several minutes, he spoke with his own defiance.

"To eliminate a young girl strictly because her assumed purpose is null and void is abominable! It is murder! Why not let her leave?"

Just then, a loud thud was heard.

Father demanded that his son sit and be still while he checked out the situation.

Both he and Mr. Leighton approached the door cautiously. Father opened the door and saw Constance lying on the floor. Her eyes were closed and her breathing was shallow. They both passed knowing glances.

The door was quickly closed while Mr. Leighton and Zachary remained in the library. The older gentlemen explained that a maid had a fainting spell while dusting.

A footman was called and Constance was carried back to her room.

Zachary's father re-entered the library and said that the maid was doing better and there was no need for concern. Since when was Father concerned in the least bit about the house staff? Zachary was skeptical as to his father's true words of care.

This minor distraction wasn't going to sidetrack Zachary from his objective. He knew he needed to stop the school, even at the expense of his own family.

Gathering his composure, and right in step with the

subject at hand, Father stood straight at attention and looked fiercely at his son. In a brusque and concise approach, Father explained the school's reasoning, and as he spoke his face contorted and grew redder with such antagonism as Zachary had never witnessed before.

Father continued his barrage.

"An agreement is signed between the school and the member. It details requirements that are suited specifically for that member, and, it states the cost for that service.

It takes countless years in order to achieve the optimum outcome. First, we must locate and acquire young beauties whose families readily take money for that child. Frequently, we can get girls from orphanages or factories for small sums. We examine each girl for her talents, her demeanor, and especially her ability to obey.

How trainable is she? All this is not easy Zachary."

The father looked into his son's eyes hoping to see some semblance of acceptance. Instead, he witnessed his son's condemnation. He continued his lecture nonetheless.

"This school greatly benefits our country, our gentlemen, and generations to follow!

A new member comes to The Harlan School for a perfect wife who fits into his life with his needs and wants trained into a specific girl. He observes her for years and meets with us in order to ensure his satisfaction."

Harlan Leighton was acutely incensed as he observed defiance from the son. He doubted that this son was capable of toeing the line. Sitting there, he listened as the father tried to convince the son of the school's noble intentions.

"And what happens in the event a member is not satisfied with our service?" Father prodded with angry resolve.

Waiting a few moments, he answered his own question.

"The cost is split between the school and the member.

And tell me Zachary, what are we supposed to do with her then? A new member does not want someone else's discard!"

The son was astonished.

"Do we turn her into a maid at Harlan? She would not be able to perform any of those duties easily because she is not trained to do anything except to be an affluent wife!

What would the other young ladies think in relation to that turn of events? It would confuse and frighten them. Yes, it would unnerve them!"

It was exceedingly difficult for Zachary to sit and listen to these ludicrous words which glorified the school's purpose. His father positioned his hands on Zachary's shoulders and kept the son in his seat.

"Do we throw her out onto the streets? Most likely she would be noticed, and noticed by the law. They would trace her back to Harlan and that would be detrimental to The Harlan School. Questions would be raised. Can you not see that?"

The father trembled with increasing hostility.

"Do we allow her to stay at Harlan for the rest of her life, and at our cost? This is a business, not a charity.

Zachary, it is rare that a transaction does not come to

fruition. It is rare son. I cannot remember the last time we had that situation. Our success rate is phenomenal. That is why we are still in business.

Harlan Leighton knows and takes care of business!"

Zachary was horrified, not only at the precision and ruthlessness of the school, but that his father and grandfather had something to do with this brutality.

And who was this man in this room, this Harlan Leighton? What hold did he have over his father?

His thoughts, once more, turned to this mans' last name – Leighton. Could Lacey be a part of his sick and twisted life? What could this mean for her future? He needed to get back to the school and get her out of there, get her to safety.

The rush of thoughts kept racing.

Marrying Constance was decidedly wrong for both of them. He needed to correct the problem. The problem being the school!

His father broke Zachary's concentration, and stated with stern expression "You see now, do you not, why you will marry Constance? She is yours!"

Zachary stood up and looked at both men vehemently and severely. He headed out of the library, and as he got to the door, with mulish resolve, turned to both men and said "NO!"

CHAPTER 11

HIS DECISION

As soon as he walked out of the library, Zachary knew there'd be hell to pay. He never disobeyed his father. Avoiding Constance was paramount at this point and he headed to his bedroom in order to think this whole thing through. A knock at the door broke his concentration, and as his sister entered the room, he was more anxious than ever.

For her protection, he would tell her nothing. He wasn't even sure of his own safety. The expressions on those two men's faces were cold, bitter cold, with a determination he hadn't seen before.

Who was this Harlan Leighton? The school's name was Harlan. Was it his school? He was in business with his grandfather! Why hadn't he met him before? He now realized why the name "Leighton" sounded familiar. He must have heard his father mention it.

Zachary's nervous disposition was easily seen by his sister. Did the conversation in the library have any bearing on his demeanor, she inquired? He convinced her that she was only supposing things, and actually, he was just tired from the Philadelphia trip.

A few minutes later, after his sister left the room, there came another knock on the door. It was Zachary's father and he was tyrannical. He came into the room with the force of a hurricane, accusing Zachary of every negative trait one could have, and threatening to disown him unless this marriage took place.

The two argued for an hour with Zachary holding tight to his decision.

No marriage with Constance!

With energized vigor, Zachary asserted with strong conviction that The Harlan School wasn't a finishing school, but in fact was a factory set up for the sale of the "perfect wife" to whoever could pay the fee, with no consideration of the young ladies feelings or desires.

His father's silence was the final confirmation.

Abruptly, without contemplation, Zachary informed his father that he'll tell authorities about the school. He didn't know his father's full participation at Harlan, and didn't care, and continued to spew out his own brand of truth.

Father had brushed aside his son's questions with perfect indignation until his son threatened to expose the school's true purpose. His father's face, as Zachary had witnessed earlier, became taut and twisted. Zachary's whole being trembled. A pointed finger pierced his chest as his father began to shout.

"You have no idea who you are dealing with. You cannot make this decision lightly. You must think this through further, longer, and deeper."

Except, Zachary's mind was made up. Tomorrow he would talk with the local constable and start on a path to free the young ladies at The Harlan School.

Zachary's father walked out shaking his head and clenching his fists. He could read his son's mind.

* * * * * *

A few hours later Zachary could hear his father and this Leighton fellow arguing in the library. They were attempting to keep their voices quiet, but to no avail, and he knew they were talking about him.

Constance hadn't been seen since mid-afternoon. Neither Zachary's mother nor his siblings had seen her, and neither had any of the servants. Where could she be? He felt sorrow when thinking of her and knew she must be aware of his feelings. The guilt was useless and served no purpose except to distract him from his mission.

Would he be stopped? How?

Would he indeed have the courage to follow this through?

Just before dinner Father requested that Zachary come outside and show Harlan Leighton the estate grounds. He explained that no matter what their differences were at this juncture, Zachary owed him this courtesy, and that tomorrow Zachary could do whatever his conscience dictated.

His father's anger appeared to have softened and that caused Zachary to relax his guard. He followed his father out to the lush green gardens east of the house.

They were waiting for Mr. Leighton when his father

quietly spoke.

"The decision you made this afternoon has severe consequences. Do you understand that?"

Zachary replied instantly, "Yes, I do. Without any doubt, it is the right decision. You cannot force young ladies to marry in this day and age!"

Father looked wounded, and could only shake his head.

Mr. Leighton was now walking towards them and a large burly man was beside him. Zachary didn't recognize this man.

The two men were now only a few feet away.

Again, the father pleaded with his son to change his mind.

"You are my son, and I need you, so please re-think this whole situation."

Zachary, without wavering or faltering, shook his head from side to side. His father looked at his son with disappointment, anguish and trepidation as he grumbled, "Consequently, your decision against me, has been made."

His father's face was ashen, and Zachary became agitated and distressed as he watched the burly man swiftly come towards him with some sort of object in his hand.

The father grabbed his son's arms.

Zachary immediately understood, and cried out in horror and disbelief.

"Father!"

Through his eyes, the world had slowed down, the

birds stopped singing, the trees were no longer swaying and Zachary was frozen in an instant of time.

At that moment the burly man wielded a heavy iron bar above Zachary's head, and struck violently.

Zachary fell to the ground, lifeless.

CHAPTER 12

HER LAST DAYS

Constance awoke with a heavy heart. Last night she was quite sure that Zachary had no interest in her.

She knew time was on her side and perhaps he'd come to care for her and want her in his life, as promised by the mentors. Besides, she was a beauty, talented, and just right for an aspiring young executive. And, it was uncanny how much they had in common. Her love for horses and Beethoven was only the beginning of their shared interests.

Constance often reminisced to the evening she went to the city's music hall and watched from the balcony as the orchestra performed Beethoven's 5th. What an experience! She had never visited the city before, and her head was filled with all the images and sounds.

Sitting at the table this morning at The Harlan School, she waited for Zachary to enter the dining room. He never came and she wondered why. Could he be eating in his room or eating in the guest dining room? Was he avoiding her? She knew she had developed deep feelings for him, and reasoned that they could grow stronger if he'd only reciprocate, even a little.

Perhaps she'd see him at lunch.

Later that day, lunch was served with no sign of him there either. Walking into the West Parlor, she sank into the settee and wept. No one was around and she felt alone and silly. He never gave any indication other than friendship and she knew this. Yet, she couldn't stop thinking about him.

A familiar footman came into the parlor and motioned for her to follow him. Constance was always obedient, so she followed the footman. They proceeded up the west stairway and down the hall to the mentor's offices, where she was instructed to sit until called.

Sitting there for several minutes, she became restless. She felt something was wrong, or something was going to happen that could cause her distress. Did Zachary complain? If so, what were his complaints? That she was friendly?

Putting these notions out of her mind, she recalled her first days at the school and how wonderful they had been. The bazaar was so much fun, but the school was especially a safe haven.

No one could hurt her here.

Mr. Olson opened his door, and instructed her to take a seat in his office saying he'd be right back. She saw his kind face, sat down with renewed optimism, and willed herself to be the mature young lady Mr. Olson expected her to be. He re-entered the room and sat in the chair next to Constance, took her hand and asked how she was doing, if she was feeling well. She immediately relaxed, and answered in her polite way that she was doing and feeling well, thank you.

"I have been told that you like a particular young man. Is this true?" he asked.

Constance was unsure how to answer. Being only sixteen and a half, she was still learning to understand life, men, marriage, and what the school expected of her.

"Yes, Mr. Olson, I met a young man and I care for him very much," she explained.

"Good," he said with a smile and a wink.

"Constance, you will be going on a trip today, and you will meet your young man at his home!"

Could this be true? Constance was overjoyed, and at a loss for words, and gently hugged the Headmaster.

* * * * * *

She'd never been on a train before. Never even saw one and now she was heading to the station to board a machine that would bring her closer to Zachary. The sheer size of the engine and the cars were overwhelming. When instructed to board, she became frightened but soon after was resolute and boarded with her head held high.

Once the train pulled out of the station, the back and forth motion caused some nausea; she felt she might throw up, but didn't. The older gentleman traveling with her said nothing. Constance saw him as a mean ogre – someone you wouldn't want to know if you had a choice. To her, he appeared to be the most unfriendly person she ever met.

It was a necessity, she knew, to travel with a chaperon, and understood this gentleman was serving that purpose. Harlan School young ladies never travelled alone.

Eventually lulled by the rhythmic motions of the train, Constance allowed herself to relax and enjoy the experience. The spectacular views from her window took her breath away.

Eventually the train came to its final destination, Jersey City, New Jersey, and all passengers de boarded. Street transportation was waiting and she and the older gentlemen stepped up into the carriage as their luggage was secured. As the carriage pulled out of the station, Constance was captivated by the activity occurring all around. Such a contrast to the order required at school.

They stopped for the first night at a quaint inn a short distance from the station, and her bags were brought to her room. She understood from the driver that she'd be staying here the night, leaving early in the morning. The trip was scheduled for three more days.

Falling asleep was proving difficult, perhaps due to the unfamiliar surroundings. So Constance lit the bedside candles, propped up her pillows, and began to read the book she had placed earlier on the bed stand.

Her mind though was a flutter, and it was difficult for her to keep her attention on the story she was reading. Blowing out the candles, she laid down and let her mind travel freely. Sleep finally came.

There was a soft knock at the door and a woman's voice sweetly said "Breakfast in thirty minutes." Constance arose from bed immediately, and washed in the basin that had been prepared for her. After dressing, she went downstairs to eat breakfast.

The older gentleman wasn't there and she was glad of that. As it turned out, she was the only one eating.

A stagecoach sat proudly at the inn's entrance and would be their transportation for the rest of the trip. A long, bumpy, dusty ride lay ahead. And as the stagecoach was pulled along the uneven roads, Constance felt the weight of a throbbing headache. And as on the train the day before, felt the misery of nausea.

The older gentleman, as she predicted, said not a word.

Finally, after three days of discomfort on the road and two nights at charming inns, they arrived in Boston. A carriage was waiting to take them to their final destination.

They arrived at the Dorsey mansion late in the evening, and lights were flickering in numerous windows. The footman offered his hand for Constance to hold while she stepped down from the stagecoach, and continued to hold her hand as she ascended the stairs to the front door. Another footman opened the doors and the Housekeeper showed her to her bedroom.

It was a large space, and she marveled at the notion that she alone might be sleeping here. She had been somewhat uneasy sleeping at the inns on this trip, as she had never slept alone in a room.

The beautiful fabrics, the matching wallpaper and the magnificence of the manor, stimulated her appetite and she looked forward to exploring the rest of the house and grounds. She loved horses and rode as often as she could back at school, and was hoping she'd get a chance to ride here.

Her breakfast had been brought to her on a tray and was utterly delicious. She had never been treated to breakfast in bed before and was now certain this was the best way to start the day.

While a ladies maid was unpacking her suitcases Constance noticed there were no suitcases or clothes other than her own. Was she not sharing this room with someone else, she asked the maid, and was delighted to hear that the room was exclusively hers.

The maid relayed to Constance that she was to relax in her room until called for lunch, and further, that she'd come back to help her dress. The lunch was to be a grand lunch and appropriate attire was required.

Several hours later, Constance was deciding which dress to wear. She'd been taught well, and chose her favorite one. There was a knock at the door, and the maid entered. "That is the perfect dress Miss Constance," the maid stated with sincerity.

After making sure all was in its proper place, Constance descended the stairs and entered the dining room, where she was instructed to sit in the chair opposite the older gentleman.

In walked the family, and then Zachary. Constance looked at Zachary with warm affection and he looked at her, she thought, with a look of contempt. Feeling despair, she questioned why she was here.

The lunch went well enough with conversation and

small talk that kept the lunch interesting. After dessert, Constance was shown the manor with its exquisite adornments, and the magnificent grounds by Zachary's mother and sister. These two ladies were gracious and hospitable and Constance was grateful for their kindness.

Getting back to her room, Constance sat on the quilted chair by the bay window and sobbed. The look on Zachary's face at lunch was anything but welcoming. A few minutes had passed when she heard a knock at the door. She opened the door with apprehension.

"Are you comfortable," the head of the house, Mr. Dorsey solicited.

"If you need anything, please let us know," he added.

The father appeared benevolent and considerate as he explained that his son was hard-headed, and for her not to lose sight of what was yet feasible for both she and Zachary. Maybe this could work out and she'd be with Zachary after all. A smile sneaked across Constance's cheeks as Mr. Dorsey opened the door, and walked into the hallway.

She was now in a state of grace.

A short time later, Constance decided to walk around the gardens on her own, and was walking down the stairs when she heard men arguing. It was heated and she heard her name mentioned. Quietly she walked to the library to hear more and pressed her ear to the library door. She recognized the voices of Mr. Dorsey, Zachary, and the older gentleman – her chaperon.

She knew her behavior was wrong, but she couldn't resist the temptation of hearing what was being said.

Were they arguing over her? Perhaps Zachary wasn't eager to be with her. Was his father wrong?

The conversation took a peculiar turn, and Constance began to question everything in her life. What did Zachary mean by saying she was a dupe. That she had been taught to be the quintessential wife – not questioning her husband, not questioning his motives, and not questioning anything!

She obeyed. That was it. And if she didn't, she'd pay a heavy price.

What did they mean by *elimination*?

Constance began to shiver.

Was she able to grasp the enormity of what was being said?

They were easily expendable!

Constance was now trembling and holding back tears as best she could. The reality of the conversation behind that door was too much: her heart pounded; she felt cold. Suddenly Constance fainted directly against the door. The thud was heard by the three men in the room.

* * * * * *

Constance was groggy when she awoke. A beam of light was streaming into the room from between the partly open curtains.

Lying there, she wondered how she got into bed; she couldn't remember doing so. Was this not mid-afternoon still? She then felt pain on the side of her head, and stroked what seemed to be a large welt. How did that occur?

She leaned over to the bedside table to pour a glass of

water and noticed a large burly man sitting at the end of her bed! The man was staring at her, with a malicious grin. At first she thought she must be half asleep and perhaps dreaming, but a few moments later she knew the truth as a memory came flooding back.

The library! The voices!

And she remembered.

Quickly throwing off the coverlet and jumping out of bed, Constance attempted to reach the door as the terror escalated. The burly man blocked that escape as he decreed with a degree of satisfaction, "Do not bother screaming young lady – no one is around to hear you!"

He had already laid plans to hide his prey in the bed, beneath the puffy coverlet, so no one would see her if they looked into her room.

Constance glanced around the room in disbelief.

Tears welled up.

Shaking and trembling, she could only watch as this man forcefully placed his rough hands on her delicate neck. An instant later, he tightened his grip until she stopped breathing.

CHAPTER 13

BEING SEVENTEEN

Today was her first afternoon soiree. Many of the girls have a soiree at fifteen or sixteen years of age. Lacey's time was now. You don't question the mentors.

Her birthday was a few days ago, and she was still in the throes of the birthday fun. She received a new dress, a new bonnet, and parasol. Of course each was a pale shade of green, her favorite color. Wearing the new clothes today, she knew she looked outstanding.

Lacey had grown up with striking features, a tall stature of slender grace, and a voice smooth as silk.

She was past those adolescent days of crushes and lost loves and looked to the future with optimism. Lacey even loved singing and was convinced that her voice was at least adequate, perhaps even good. Her mentors had said her voice was special. Practicing dutifully, she became quite proficient.

Her favorite composer was Beethoven, but this afternoon, at the musical soiree, she was directed to sing "Non so piu cosa son" from Mozart's "Marriage of

Figaro." It wasn't her favorite aria, but she had learned not to question her teacher's choices.

This was to be her first public appearance!

Until then, she was relaxing in her room anticipating who she'd meet this night. A young handsome fellow no doubt: tall and slender with warm inviting eyes, a smile that beckoned her heart to his.

She wanted to wear her mother's ribbon in her hair – a special ribbon for a special day. Opening the drawer with the petticoats, she retrieved her sachet.

As she was looking for the ribbon, she spotted her mother's diary that had been sitting next to the sachet. She had been proud of herself all these years for not reading those private words, and also for not dwelling on nonsense such as dubious coins and mysterious shadows.

Recently though, now that she was seventeen, she had convinced herself that reading the diary could broaden her understanding of her parents, and perhaps the world. And besides, her heart had been broken by Zachary and she felt that this life experience, a lost love, had prepared her for reading her mother's words.

Lacey placed the ribbon on the bureau to be put in her hair later. It was a beautiful ribbon, her mother's favorite color, a pale shade of violet. The ribbon would accent her hair beautifully, and she'd have a sense that he mother was in the room, listening as she sang.

She sat down on her bed with the diary in hand, feeling with her fingers the gold embossed letters on the front. Opening to the first page, Lacey took a deep breath. She felt like she was entering a forbidden world, and began to read.

Within the first few pages Lacey learned that her mother started the diary soon after she was married. It had been a birthday present from her mother. Prior to that, Mother never wrote in it before because she was waiting for life to give her something to write about. The marriage should have given her interesting and enjoyable events and occasions to note in her diary. Instead, shortly after she started writing, she was aware that her diary was filled with nothing but sadness.

For the most part, she wrote daily until the day she died. It somehow helped her get through the day, and the night.

Since the record was uneventful for many years, Lacey began to skip pages, yet was still able to glean from the writings that her mother was shielding her truest feelings regarding her marriage.

Gradually, there was a new and menacing presence in her mother's life, and it caused much apprehension. She didn't write about it in great detail. Lacey could glean only that this presence was an older gentleman, at first staying in the shadows.

The more she read the more familiar this gentleman became. Her mother wrote of her confusion.

Friday, May 16, 1864

I thought by now the war, after these many years, would be over. It is not, and it is still going strong.

It was a beautiful clear day today. The

rain had stopped, and it warmed up. I think there will be a full moon tomorrow night.

With the break in the weather, I went into town.

That gentleman, I call the ghost, came out of the shadows and talked with me at the Linen Shop. I have seen him before but we never spoke and he always kept his distance.

My eyes were drawn immediately to the gold ring he was wearing. I tried not to stare. It had tiny diamonds inlayed in a horse shoe design. The ring was so sparkly. I never saw a piece of jewelry reflecting such beautiful colors. It was so unique that I doubt if I will ever forget the design and exquisiteness of that ring, or ever see another like it.

This gentleman was such a tall and statuesque man that he stood out from the rest.

He asked how the boys were doing and said he knew my father when I was quite young. There is such mystery surrounding this gentleman. He seems kind. He never asks for anything except a friendly gesture when we see each other.

He said his name was Harry Lawrence. I never thought he was telling me his real name. I do not know why I thought this. Maybe it was the way he said it - with such reservation.

Now I am pregnant with my third child,

and he dotes on me. I often wonder what he really wants from me. I have invited him back to the house to meet my family, and he has declined with a decisive excuse. I no longer invite him.

He does look familiar to me. Always has. Once I imagined that he looked just like my husband - how strange."

Lacey stopped reading and laid back onto her pillow, while her head was in a whirl. These were her mother's words, her mother's reactions to life. Tears crept down her cheeks and she reached for a crisp clean handkerchief.

The gentleman in the diary seemed familiar to her, but why should he? Lacey's phantom never leaves the shadows and mother's gentleman was in full view.

Lacey knew very little of her mother's life before she met Papa. And now, the diary spoke to Lacey of her mother's parents, and their fondness and affection for their only child.

Unfortunately for Mother, she married the wrong man.

Their life's circumstances (mother and daughter) unfolded in opposite ways. Mother's life was good until she was married. Daughter's life was bad until she entered The Harlan School.

Rueby knocked on the door as expected, and Lacey politely voiced "come in."

She put the diary under her bed to be read later.

Facing each other, they both looked at one another

with sheer delight as to how beautiful they both were – so grown up and sophisticated.

They both walked into the hall with great anticipation.

* * * * * *

Rueby was nervous and apprehensive. Would she talk too much, or perhaps be a bore with nothing interesting to say?

Today, remembering her lessons was imperative!

Lacey tried to put Rueby's fears to rest and said emphatically "We are now seventeen and I want to meet the world!"

It had taken more than a year for Lacey to trust her feelings again. She trusted Zachary, and from that she received nothing but pain. That he was at Harlan to meet a wife that was pre-determined for him – well, that was ridiculous.

And more importantly, for him to have left unexpectedly without saying good bye was cruel. How could she have been deceived so easily? Now, trust is not a commodity she gives away easily.

This change in her nature saddened her, but she had to be less vulnerable.

Lacey and Rueby walked into the parlor and had a seat by the Muselar harpsichord. The room was filled with Harlan young ladies, and all types of gentlemen of all ages and sizes, and many speaking foreign languages.

Mr. Keane approached Lacey and motioned for her to stand. She moved to the spot that was designated the day before, composed herself, took several deep breaths, nodded to the accompanist, and sang Non so piu cosa son.

She was poised, confident, and most of all, she was having fun.

She was beaming!

After a great deal of clapping and applause, she sat back down next to Rueby.

"What a voice you have Lacey! I had no idea your voice was so beautiful. Angels! Angels!" exclaimed Rueby lovingly.

"You gave me chills!"

Lacey blushed.

Several minutes later a gentleman approached and took a seat next to Rueby. After a short conversation he asked her to walk in the gardens, leaving Lacey alone.

Lacey surveyed the room watching and observing. But what was she looking for?

It was peculiar to Lacey that the pairing between the men and the young ladies happened so quickly. She expected a gathering where everyone met one another, and perhaps, if you were lucky, you could meet someone that furthered your interest. Yet, here and now, Lacey was the only one alone.

And the room was emptying quickly. Lacey had expected an evening of conversation, an evening of getting to know the outside world. Had most of the young ladies met these men before? And if so, why hadn't she?

Sitting there for several minutes, she remembered the conversation with Zachary, and how he said he was there to meet Constance. He wasn't there to meet Harlan's young ladies. He was there to meet his "wife!" This made no sense to Lacey and she had to dismiss it.

Still, even now, she can see the torment on his face.

A few more minutes passed and Mr. Russell walked in.

"Lacey, I see you are here alone. Do not be discouraged. Harlan has great plans for you!"

As he turned to leave, she responded "what plans?" and he quietly suggested "in time Lacey, in time."

105

CHAPTER 14

QUESTIONS

Rueby was ecstatic. She could hardly contain herself as she tried to tell her best friend everything.

"He and I have so much in common Lacey. It was easy for me to talk with him. He lives in a small town in Ohio, owns a factory, is a widower, and has one child who he loves dearly. He must be a kind and considerate man. I hope to see him again."

Lacey glared in disbelief. Rueby doesn't know this man. Nevertheless, she can't stop talking about him. Didn't she learn anything from Lacey's own encounter with Zachary?

"Take your time Rueby," Lacey reprimanded with sincere disquiet.

Noticing Rueby's pendent dangling on a chain around her neck, Lacey could only smile. There was an offer to each young lady to have the antique relic cleaned and polished and attached to a pretty chain. They all loved the idea except for Lacey. She wanted it as is.

If it were only true that this relic had great value she

contemplated. She had given this much thought, and had long since forgiven the school for their little white lie regarding the coins. Reasoning that they only wanted to bring joy to their charges, Lacey hoped that the gift was actually a touch of kindness. The school perhaps bought many of these coins from the bazaar.

With that revelation, Lacey's body quivered.

The bazaar!

Was there a connection between the bazaar and The Harlan School?

Rueby could see the intense change in her friend's countenance.

"Are you all right?" she inquired with heartfelt attention.

"I am fine. I was only thinking of your new gentleman friend," Lacey explained.

Getting her attention back on Rueby, Lacey looked at her friend earnestly and begged her to go slowly with her man from Ohio. But would she? Rueby had always been impulsive and impetuous.

"No need to be troubled Lacey. I will take good care of my feelings," Rueby confidently averred as she glided from the room.

As soon as the door shut, Lacey's mind immediately turned to the bazaar.

All these questions and no answers were making her head spin. Didn't one of the older girls tell her she also went to a bazaar? And, didn't Rueby? Was it that unusual for young girls to go to the local bazaar? Alone! Did the school run the bazaar? Why? Were they looking for young girls? Young girls with indifferent or heartless families? Young girls from destitute families? Young girls who were orphaned?

That idea stopped her breathing for a moment. Was the bazaar a place to observe young girls? Is that why the gentleman gave her a ride home?

Did he pay Papa for her?

Did Papa actually sell her?

Did Rueby's father sell Rueby?

Did all the girls' fathers sell them?

And did orphanages sell their waifs?

This was a terrifying calculation. The ramifications were too awful to bear and she shook off this appalling suspicion. She had no choice!

To steady her mind, she sat down on her bed and picked up the diary. As she read, she could feel once more the intense pain and formidable loss of hope in her mother's words. After reading many pages, the words went in an ominous direction.

Monday, September 26, 1864

This was a day I will never forget. I have to write down the whole story, otherwise it will haunt me.

I went to the linen shop this afternoon for some fabric to make a new coverlet for the crib. I bought a piece of wool fabric which should be warm enough for the winter.

As I was walking out, that "Mr. Lawrence" was crossing the street. He spotted, and approached me. He asked if I would have tea with him at Miss Diane's Tea Room. I had never been there before and I was especially concerned that my appearance was not suitable. He put aside my concerns, and said I looked fine for the occasion.

As we were sipping the most delicious tea I have ever tasted, he began to tell me how much he looked forward to seeing me. I realized how much I enjoyed seeing him too.

Our conversations were always interesting. We talked about things I could never discuss with my husband, or anyone else I knew. He must be very educated and always challenged my mind.

I knew he would be out of my life at some point, and I knew I would miss our exchanges.

Today, our talk took a grave turn.

He professed his love and admiration for me, and even though he was much older, thought we could be happy together.

I was shocked, and had no idea he had those feelings.

He explained further that he had never met any woman that brought out of him such passions and desires.

Looking at him in disbelief, I explained that even if I felt the same, I was married, had two children, and was expecting a third child!

He shook his head and said "Yes, I know." Silence prevailed.

He reached over and took hold of my hand. I can remember exactly what he said next.

"I am going to tell you a story that will surprise you.

I did not know your father as I once told you. I knew your husband, and I know what a miserable character he is. I have observed him at a distance. He has not changed since he was a child."

"Since he was a child," I said. "How do you know this?"

This opened a deluge and he explained in a rather mundane tone that he was my husband's father.

"My husband's father," I said incredulously!

He explained that fatherhood gave him the right to interfere in his son's life.

I did not know what to say or how to react. We thought the father was long gone, and now here he is.

Asking me to be with him!

"Your husband does not deserve a lady as fine as yourself. Leave the boys with him. I will adopt the newborn."

He said all of this so casually and matter of fact. I could not believe what I was hearing.

"Divorces can be bought, and I will pay off a legislator, or judge, if need be, and we will wed once it is finalized," he added assuredly.

At this point all I could do was stare at him. He noticed my apprehension and held my hand even tighter.

I drew in a deep breath, perhaps the deepest breath I had ever taken, and actually got a little dizzy. With as much politeness as I could muster, I told Mr. Lawrence... no Mr. Leighton, that his offer was generous, but that I did not have the same feelings towards him, and could not be with him romantically.

He let go of my hand roughly, and glowered, as his demeanor instantly became threatening, and I became fearful as he spewed,

"You are making the greatest mistake of your life. You and your unborn child could have had perfection - a life of grandeur. And instead, you are choosing a life of poverty and hardship."

He was right! I was choosing to stay with my husband and our family on our paltry farm. I knew this life. I knew my husband, and what to expect.

I was choosing the familiar. It seemed safer.

Suddenly, he rose from the table, took coins from his pocket to pay for the tea, and leaned towards me, putting his hands on my shoulders, squeezing tightly, and whispered into my ear,

"You will say nothing of this to your

husband! If you do, I will know! And if you do say anything to him, there will be consequences to pay.

Do not test me!

Do you understand?"

There was no uncertainty as to what he meant. He threatened me, my children, and his son.

My voice quaked as I said

"I do understand."

I watched him leave the tea room and wondered why it was so important that my husband not know that his father was alive. But I am sure he had his reasons, and I was not going to question him.

This entire episode will never be written about again.

It ends here!

Tuesday, September 27, 1864

I picked up the diary to write. But I cannot. I am not sure when I will write again.

Monday, December 5, 1864

I will be having this baby soon. I have decided to call her Lacey if it is a girl, after my mother, or Jeremiah, after my father, if it is a boy.

Sunday, December 11, 1864

The wife from a farm on the other side of

town has been looking in on me these past few weeks. Before that, we have never exchanged even a hello, but one day she knocked at the door saying she knew I was expecting a child and asked if she could help in any way. She seemed to know a great deal about me, which at first was unsettling, but I set aside any misgivings. Town gossip I suppose. She says very little about herself, but I am grateful for the company. Her circumstances are more desperate than ours and they have much less income than we do, and their only two sons are at war.

Through her, I have sent a message to the mid-wife to come immediately.

My labor is getting more intense.

The mid-wife has not come. It has been hours. I am so frightened. I am here all alone. I must keep writing to take the edge off this pain.

But I cannot write anymore.

Please God, help me. Help me!

* * * * * *

A healthy baby girl was delivered.

Baby Lacey was all cleaned and washed and placed gently in her crib. Her mother's eyes were closed and her hands folded on her chest. The mid-wife was waiting for the father to come home and when he did, she got ready to leave. He didn't recognize her, as Mrs. Scholl had delivered his boys.

Prior to the father coming home, the mid-wife cleaned

and dressed the mother in the high collar gown that she had brought with her, for the funeral. She covered the bruised throat with make-up, and the finger marks and neck bruising couldn't be seen at all.

It was a good job.

All of this, of course, wasn't known to Lacey. She only knew her mother had died in child birth.

Reading her mother's last words in the diary caused Lacey to weep, and she was surprised at this reaction. She supposed she loved her mother. Was that possible?

This diary posed questions, and more questions, with no answers. Could she trust the words of her mother? Perhaps those words in the diary are exaggerated, and were nothing more than a sad and fearful woman seeing more trouble than what actually existed.

Was her recall accurate?

This man may have been her father's father, but what did that mean? It probably meant nothing. Papa was an ogre, at the very least, and his father may have known this. Crossing moral lines, he wanted to bestow a good and decent life for his son's wife. It was clear that the son wasn't providing any of that.

Was the old man wrong? It appeared that he did know his son's propensities.

But then again, did he actually threaten the lives of her family? If he did, that would be unforgiveable.

Lacey smiled as she realized the irony in all of this. Despite everything, she ended up at a remarkable school.

And the similarity between the old man in her mother's diary and the man Lacey sees in her shadows?

Well, coincidence perhaps. More to the point, why would her grandfather hover in the shadows? And how would he not be seen at Harlan, since surely they'd catch any stranger trespassing on the grounds?

No, her phantom couldn't be her grandfather. Most likely he disappeared into oblivion, never to be heard from or seen again once Mother turned down his proposal.

Besides, Mother's phantom came out of the shadows, while Lacey's hasn't in these many years.

Realistically, her mystery, most likely, was imagined – or perhaps as Mr. Russell suggested, was simply a maid going about her duties.

Yet, on a deeper level, she didn't think it was.

She'd see him out of the corner of her eye, over there, obscured.

She'd have told Zachary. She'd planned to.

Oh why did she read this diary!

Between the diary and her growing belief that there was a conspiracy at the school, Lacey questioned her sanity. How could any of this be true? It was too fantastic.

She sat silent, and after a few minutes, scolded herself. It was time, once and for all, to let go of these implausible ideas – they are nothing but a waste of time.

Mr. Russell too would be scolding her for these delusions. Life was better now since she had left Zachary in the past, and she wanted life to be good.

It needed to be good.

Lacey put the diary back, under the petticoats, smiled

at the coin with no resentment or foreboding, put on her
shawl and went to dinner

CHAPTER 15

RUEBY'S MR. BADER

Dinner the night before was customary, save Rueby's non-stop chatter concerning Mr. Bader from Ohio. He was perfect. She was in love. Lacey regarded Rueby as being childish and unrealistic. Until she knew him better, and was more familiar with his way of life, she should tread lightly. Rueby, of course, deemed Lacey ridiculous for her lack of romanticism.

"Protect yourself!" Lacey reproached.

"You and I have known each other for years, and a few days and a few chance meetings are too short a time to know anyone well. Remember, after a couple of days, I thought I knew Zachary," she further clarified.

Rueby looked right through Lacey, now thinking her utterly dismal and senseless. What did she know?

One love affair doesn't produce an expert on love!

Besides, Rueby knew she'd be spending more time with Mr. Bader before he leaves. She'll discover all of his quirks, his likes and dislikes. They already had so much in common.

Even with her concern for Rueby, this morning Lacey offered the world a smiling face – no questions, no sour mood. She'd be grateful to the school, her teachers and mentors. No dark perceptions allowed!

And after lunch, there'd be another soiree, more to her liking, she hoped.

Sitting and talking with a young man, or any gentleman, she expected, would be fun and entertaining. She'd wear a different dress today, a different color, because perhaps her dress yesterday was too formal for the occasion. This was a soiree after all, not the Grand Gala.

Perhaps her hair was pulled back too severely.

Today she wasn't going to allow any melancholy feelings to enter her mind. Yet the nagging judgements pushed through and took hold again. She remembered yesterday's soiree clearly: it appeared that each gentleman deliberately went to a particular young girl. And that particular girl wasn't approached by any other gentleman. It was as if that young girl had been reserved for that man. That simply couldn't be. Utterly unbelievable!

What did Zachary say? He was here to meet his "wife?" A young lady he'd never met before. All of this was weighing on Lacey, once more.

She stopped washing and placed the wash cloth and soap next to the basin, scolding herself, in Mr. Russell's stead.

"Why are you thinking such inane thoughts?" she imagined him exclaiming.

The diary, the phantom, the conspiracy, and now

suspecting the true nature of Rueby's Mr. Bader!

Her imaginings were too powerful!

* * * * *

Mr. Bader had come to call on Rueby, who was dressed in her finest attire, with small daisies adorning her hair. He was quite handsome in his dark brown suit with his dark brown hair and dark brown eyes. The juxtaposition of his dark clothes and features was striking in contrast to her sky blue dress with its lavender sash and bodice, and especially her radiant porcelain skin, deep blue eyes, and the soft amber color of her silken hair.

They were a striking pair.

Yesterday they walked through the gardens, and today they'll be together walking serenely around the pond admiring its tranquility.

Rueby believed Mr. Bader to be a considerate man. He always held her hand when she was unsteady. He was always doting on her, watching her. At times his constant observation unnerved her, and she reasoned it to be simple curiosity.

Today nonetheless, there was a hint of distance between them, more distance than she would have liked. Today he was preoccupied, less talkative, less kind.

Yes, less kind.

They were halfway around the pond and she had slipped on a small rock and twisted her ankle ever so slightly, and she winced. His lack of care surprised her.

He simply watched as she hobbled to a small bench and watched as she took off her shoe. She examined the ankle and it looked and felt fine, just slightly bruised.

Putting her shoe back on, and lacing it up, she stood beside the bench and hoped for a hand. But none came. Mr. Bader appeared to be lost in thought as he peered out onto the pond, seemingly disinterested in Rueby's dilemma. She put weight on the ankle and it did support her with only slight pain.

"We will have someone look at that immediately," he remarked. For a second, she hoped the aloofness she encountered at the pond had nothing to do with her. Perhaps he received disturbing news this morning.

But to Rueby's dismay, brought on by Mr. Bader's tone and actions, she quickly developed the impression that he was caring for a prized cow – rather than herself!

He walked slightly ahead of her as she slowly hobbled along.

He reached the door, waited for her, and opened it. Was this small gesture a show of kindness? With a slight limp, she entered the school and thanked him for holding open the door. No response. At this point she wondered what had gone wrong. They had gotten along well yesterday.

"What have I done, Mr. Bader, to upset you?" she asked inquisitively.

And with no hesitation Mr. Bader answered.

"Yesterday I was getting to know you. You are not exactly as I expected, but you are tolerable. This morning I am only reacting to that fact."

His response caused an avalanche of dread.

In that instant, Rueby knew Mr. Bader wasn't who she thought he was. Lacey was right. So right! What made this discovery bearable was that Rueby needn't see him again. Maybe she'd meet someone else this afternoon – hopefully.

* * * * * *

Rueby was told that her ankle would heal soon. It was wrapped in gauze and she was given a small cane for support. Afterwards she sat in the sun room with a cup of tea. Soon afterwards, Mr. Russell came in and invited her to follow him and they both walked slowly to his office.

After they both sat down, Mr. Russell explained that Mr. Bader was taking her for a carriage ride this afternoon. Rueby was bewildered. She explained the change in Mr. Bader's mood between yesterday and this morning and requested not to go.

A stern scowl surfaced on Mr. Russell's face with no explanation for the mood change. Rueby quietly and respectfully uttered "Mr. Russell, Mr. Bader said he only tolerated me, so why does he want to see me? I would rather go to the afternoon soiree."

Mr. Russell glared and his lips became taut.

Composing himself, and after straightening his ascot, he sharply stated "Mr. Bader is a fine gentleman, and you should feel honored that he wants to be with you. He *does*, you know. He is a powerful man and his abruptness should be overlooked.

You will see him Rueby!"

This tone was mordacious, biting, and it frightened her.

A dismal frown crept onto her face and she stared at Mr. Russell. What else could she do? Her mind went blank and she sat limply in the chair until a knock on the door broke the room's ambiance.

"Just a moment," her mentor declared as he rose from his chair. With a degree of unexpected tenderness, Mr. Russell helped Rueby to her feet, put his arm around her for comfort and support, and accompanied her to the door.

Mr. Bader was waiting for her.

And because of her ankle, a footman was there also to carry her down the hall, through the vestibule, down the front steps and into the waiting carriage. She sat helpless, across from Mr. Bader, as she watched footmen bring luggage quickly down those same steps.

First out the door and down the steps came dark leather luggage that had the initials EB embossed with gold lettering. She knew Mr. Bader's first name was Elias, and she knew that this luggage must be his. At that point, she witnessed the luggage that she had received for her last birthday being carried down the steps. Her luggage was placed next to the carriage until his luggage had been placed properly on top. Her heart leapt as she saw gold embossed lettering now on her luggage reading RB – Rueby Bader? Was this her fate?

Lacey!

The luggage was secured and the carriage pulled away heading towards the train station – destination Ohio.

PART II   HARLAN

CHAPTER 16

HIS YOUTH

Harlan Leighton had been born into abysmal poverty. His identical twin had died at birth, and his mother sunk into a deep depression from which she never recovered. He was a bastard, as they said in those days. Truth be told, his father left town as soon as he heard the girl was with child. He couldn't even stay long enough to marry her, so the child, at the very least, would be legitimate.

His Aunt, on his mother's side, raised him the best she could. She never married, not because she didn't want to, but no man ever proposed. Aunt Theodosia spent her days studying the Bible and taught Harlan to fear the Lord and walk in His righteous path.

All this glory and virtue incensed her nephew and as he grew up he became less glorious and even less virtuous.

Getting into trouble was his daily ritual. When he wasn't pulling legs off live frogs or setting fire to someone's barn he was stealing whatever he could lay his hands on.

When he was thirteen, his aunt decided to leave, and to leave without him.

The day his aunt abandoned him, Harlan had convinced the brother and sister living next door to play a game. They were eager to play because he was a few years older, and for him to want to play with them, well, it must indicate that he liked them after all. Usually, whenever they said hello they received no response. Today, he did want to play.

The little girl, secretly, had a crush on the thirteen year old. She was shy, especially around this boy. Standing at full attention, she tried to overcome her shyness and be lively, like her brother. Oh what fun they'd all have today.

The two children listened intently and with rising excitement as their neighbor explained the game they'd play. He'd tie them up and pretend to be a bad, menacing bandit. The children snickered with glee as he placed each of them next to a tree, and secured them to the tree with rope.

He then placed the twigs he had gathered earlier at their feet. The children were still chuckling with pleasure, until they saw Harlan reach for a matchstick and light the twigs on fire.

The children started screaming and yelling for help. Harlan laughed sadistically as he watched the look of absolute terror distort the children's faces as the flames nipped at their clothes. But Harlan was thirsty, so he went to the market house down the street for a delicious cream drink, a sack posset.

Next door, Mrs. Sorenson heard the screams as she

was folding her dried clothes. She ran out the back door to see the smoke rising above the trees. Calling loudly to awaken her husband who was napping on the porch, they both ran next door. They were horrified to see the children and the flames. Frantically, they searched for buckets, collected water, and doused the fire.

The twigs hadn't been fully dry because of a recent rain, which impeded the spread and intensity of the flames. If not for this, the children surely would have been gravely burned.

As it was, each child received minor burns. The girl, however, would be burdened with a conspicuous scar on her cheek, keeping many suitors away.

When Harlan came back home, after finishing his cream drink, the Sheriff was waiting, and there was no sign of Aunt Theodosia.

Her belongings were gone, and so was she.

No note, no nothing.

The teenager felt liberated.

The Sheriff communicated to the boy that he'd be going to a home that took care of his kind, and expected the thirteen year old to obey without incident. He knew he'd be taking the boy with him and brought an extra horse that was tethered to his own. As he was getting the horse readied for the young delinquent to mount, the boy took off running. The Sheriff hastily untied the tether, but it was too late. Harlan was gone.

This was the beginning of Harlan's seething. Up to this point he'd been an angry boy, but now he was on his way to becoming an angry man.

He left town quickly by stealing a horse and rambled for years working odds jobs, not staying long in any one place.

That is, until he met and married a young girl whose family included him in their business, allowing Harlan a life much better than he deserved.

His new wife was quiet and didn't say much, which suited Harlan. The less he saw of her and talked with her the better they got along. The future was secure with an easy life that he was counting on. He'd be able to do what he wanted, when he wanted, and with whom he wanted.

As the years passed, his father-in-law became too demanding for Harlan's taste and they argued frequently.

After his father-in-law died under questionable circumstances, Harlan prepped himself to run the business. Actually, he knew he'd hire people to work the day-to-day operations, while he found ways to spend the money.

Regrettably for Harlan, his father-in-law hadn't divulged the business arrangements disclosed in his Last Will and Testament, which gave the entire business to a silent partner. The position given to Harlan – an office clerk!

More than ever, he blamed and resented his wife for this obvious condemnation of his character. Now, he'd have to work hard to take care of his wife and two children, in the same place of business he should have been able to watch others work, while enjoying a comfortable life himself.

His wife, a frail woman, was growing intolerant of his

lack of care for her and the children. She began to voice her feeling, albeit quietly and reservedly. This increased his ire. He wanted her to stop talking!

If not for the stipend she received monthly from her father's estate, he'd be gone.

The silent partner should have stayed silent. He knew nothing about running a business and only two years passed before he ran the business into the ground. The end of the business meant the end of Harlan's job. Also the monthly stipend was substantially reduced. If not for his father-in-law having set up a Trust, the money would have disappeared immediately. As it was, a stipulation allowed debtors to claim some of the cash – but thankfully not all of it. The stipend would continue but only for a short time.

Harlan knew he could have run the business far better had he been in charge. When he visualized controlling the business, he was surprised to find that it appealed to him.

Harlan was well-built and strong and the local blacksmith imagined he'd make a good apprentice at his foundry. He didn't know this young fellow very well, but knew he had fallen on hard times, and aimed to offer him a hand.

Unbeknownst to Harlan, the blacksmith's intention was solely to help Harlan's wife and children. He had known Harlan's wife since she was a child and wanted to prevent any hardship.

They agreed on wages and duties and Harlan enjoyed the foundry, for a while at least. The job and the learning were becoming dull, and Harlan knew he was meant to be the one in control, not the one controlled. And certainly Harlan would not be the one doing the labor.

This blacksmith was becoming anxious and irritated with his apprentice. One day the young man left in a hurry with no explanation, and didn't come back. The blacksmith was relieved.

He was concerned still about the family and what would happen to them. Knowing there was nothing he could do, he let the matter drop.

Harlan had taken another job in another town, and moved his family there. At first, on the surface, the job sounded good to Harlan – he'd be his own boss. That part he liked, but not the rest. Running a foundry was hard work indeed, and not for him.

Harlan abandoned his family in that town after being chased out by the Constable and the people of the town.

After that, he wandered.

CHAPTER 17

GARNER, MASSACHUSETTS

He's been described as having a charming and disarming personality. For him, it was easy to gain people's trust through deliberate manipulation. These past few years had taught him much: the vulnerabilities of people, and his own talents and nature.

Harlan knew he saw everything with a keener eye than most people. He could see through anyone, see their true nature, their faults, their flaws. He learned to take advantage of anyone or any situation that came his way.

It was his given right to do so!

Being right or wrong was of no concern to Harlan. He may have known something was wrong, at least according to what other people thought, but if it fit into his plan he did it with full volition. Conscience wasn't a part of his make-up. He had discovered the absolute truest standard of right and wrong: it was his right to do what he wanted, when he wanted, and to whom he wanted.

After abandoning his family, of which he felt no shame, he moved to New England. It was the year 1843 and he was twenty three years old.

He procured a job at the Heywood-Wakefield Furniture factory in Gardner, Massachusetts. Gardner was known as the "chair city" and the "Furniture Capital of New England." His brawn landed him the job, and those quick learning skills so innate allowed him soon to demand more pay.

He spent his days making wooden chairs of all shapes, sizes and styles. Working with the lathe was tedious, and sawdust filled his nostrils, but generally the work was not too demanding. His boss was decent enough and let his workers alone so long as the job was completed by the due date.

Harlan's always was.

Throughout his employ at the factory, he was able to watch as trees were cut down in the forests, sawed and milled. He thought this was experience that could prove beneficial to someone heading out west.

To earn extra cash, he decided to get a job at a blacksmith's helping out with the iron work. He had seen the advertisement tacked to the door for a helper when he passed by the foundry. If he could work with the iron and not the horse, he'd apply. That was, in fact, the case, and he was offered the job starting the next day.

He, of course, exaggerated his experience; he had confidence in what he knew, and he knew enough to get by.

The first day he was instructed to bend a length of iron into a circle. Then to attach spokes from a central hub to the inside of the circle. What was this contraption he was assembling? After a couple of days it looked familiar. And then it came to him. It was similar to the draisienne he had ridden in his youth.

That was an awful contraption.

This one was remarkably different. He asked the blacksmith about it and was shown one that had been completed last week. Harlan was astonished and wanted one. The blacksmith was willing to part with this bicycle for a discounted price.

Buying a horse for transportation wasn't in Harlan's tight budget. Horses were too expensive not just to purchase but also to maintain. Consequently, this bicycle was the alternative he needed to get back and forth to the factory.

He had rented a room above a cigar shop. The room was small, clean, with new wallpaper, and a new bedspread that matched the new curtains. One lone chair sat in the corner next to a small table with an oil lamp, and a picture was hanging above the bed that showed birds flying above a beach with the ocean in the background.

Not a bad room for the price.

The window opened to a little courtyard in the back of the cigar shop where patrons sat and sampled numerous varieties of tobacco that the shop had to offer. The smoke wafted into his room, which didn't disturb him in the least.

Harlan had made a plan! With these tolerable jobs, he could save enough money in two to three years to go out west. That is where he should be.

He also presumed that the West had fewer of those radical females spewing their propaganda of suffrage and women's rights. It was tiresome hearing and reading about these insufferable women, like Elizabeth Cady Stanton and her followers. Women already had the rights bestowed to their ilk; they were not entitled to more.

This mind-set, this attitude, was nothing new for Harlan. He grew up noticing that decent and respectable wives didn't question their husbands. They didn't argue; they did what they were told so there would be harmony in the household. The husband would come and go as he saw fit knowing that his wife was home taking care of the household and the children. The husband and the wife each had their own specific duty.

Wives must be obedient! Without this, the home would be chaotic.

When Harlan married, he assumed his wife would value her position, and be grateful for it. And for a while, she did seem to value her position and was grateful.

His wife began their marriage as a good, quiet, and acceptable young girl. Then she morphed into a female he didn't recognize. She had started reading any article on women's rights that she could get her hands on before Harlan found it and threw it out.

One of the first articles he found her reading was written in 1839 and discussed The Married Women's Property Acts. It was now 1841 and she had hidden it well.

His wife knew better than to argue and as he grabbed another article from her hands, she cried. She could feel her blood drain as she realized her life would be confined to these walls, with this man.

An obsession began to grow within the confines of Harlan's brain. How could modern man stop the advancement that threatened their way of life? Their home security!

He had rationalized that these modern times, with these new gadgets and inventions that helped ease a wife's burden, only inflamed their ridiculous unrest.

Marriage! He married once and couldn't imagine another go round. He'd go out west and have a new life.

Save money! That's the goal.

CHAPTER 18

GEARS, CHAINS, AND PULLEYS

Harlan had been surprised how much he enjoyed working on the mechanisms of the bicycle. He learned a great deal about mechanized machinery, and how gears and chains could work in tandem.

The "how" something worked had always been more interesting to Harlan than forging materials or assembly. Yet, unlike shoeing horses, he now found himself looking forward to stoking the pit, firing the material, and pounding out the design on the anvil. It gave him a sense of satisfaction he hadn't experienced before.

This bicycle invention was a modern asset, Harlan theorized, and wouldn't diminish the standard way of life. Not much would be changed except that a few less horses would be ridden. He didn't care that the farrier's trade could be in jeopardy with fewer horses to tend to.

On a rare day off from work, Harlan went to an arcade that had opened on the outskirts of town. He was amazed at how much he could buy for his few cents. Not like at the local shops.

Eating was an adventure in itself with all types of food at his fingertips. Choosing what to eat was difficult for he only wanted to spend a small sum and he knew he could eat all day! He opted for the sweets and ate the sticky cinnamon bun which was perfection.

Sitting on a bench under a large-leaved tree to shade the hot sun, he watched as people strolled by. They were eating, carrying prizes, or trying to keep their children in line.

Harlan expected to see more riff-raff at this arcade, but noticed most of the patrons were the upper crust of Gardner. There were definitely folks of lower means, akin to himself, dressed in their Sunday best, all cleaned and bathed.

He quickly realized how easy it was to be a voyeur, sitting here practically unnoticed, scrutinizing and inspecting the passerby's. This observation would be stored in his memory, without intention, until one day it came flooding back in one of his brilliant ideas.

After enjoying the last bite of the cinnamon bun, Harlan drifted around the arcade grounds, watching the patrons play the games. There were so many of these games, all different, yet similar in one way or another: shoot a gun at a target or throw a ball at a hole in a wood plank. All of these were tedious to Harlan.

Noticing that a number of the games had targets that moved from side to side, Harlan speculated on how the targets moved. He knew there must be some sort of mechanism. Sitting down, he wondered what mechanics were needed in order to get that movement.

Gears and chains again, just like the bicycle. Harlan wondered if he couldn't invent a better game, a game that had more interaction with the prizes – more than shooting or throwing a ball.

That's too simple!

Sitting quietly, he allowed his brain to deliberate.

"Was there a game more challenging that used gears and chains?"

Then he saw it. He saw the machine in his mind's eye. It was made of glass with all sorts of toys sitting at the bottom waiting to be snatched up, taunting the player. A large arm with a head-like attachment with teeth could grab and hold on to the toy of choice. It would have some sort of handle that the player could manipulate. But how could it be done?

The rest of the day, and while riding back to his room he imagined all aspects of the game. Could he construct it? More importantly, why should he try? The answer came quickly.

For Harlan, all things came easy, and for once, this would be a challenge!

Harlan decided to ask the blacksmith if in his spare time and using discarded supplies, he could try to make this machine. Harlan knew he was heading out west soon, and suggested that if the machine worked, he'd leave it at the foundry for customers to play. The blacksmith knew Harlan was saving monies to go west, knew of his job at the furniture factory, and wondered what spare time he'd have to work on the invention.

Even so, the blacksmith assured him that he'd hold

the game and whenever he was ready for it, Harlan could retrieve it.

Five months and many sleepless nights later, the mechanized invention worked with all its gears, chains and pulleys.

CHAPTER 19

JANUARY 24, 1848

Harlan had saved quite a sum of money. Being cheap paid off as he kept every coin except for rent and food. No extravagances. His mind had been made up and he was heading west.

By mid-March, he had already bought the necessary equipment for the long wagon train journey to California. He knew there were railroad trains that could take him a short distance, but the cost was prohibitive. A wagon train would be the mode of his transportation.

As expected, the journey was treacherous and dangerous. Harlan lived through it without a scratch. He was expecting to get to California by mid-November, and had no idea what kind of work he'd do after he arrived. The money would only last a short time. He'd need to find work quickly.

It was wet and windy when he arrived in San Francisco, on November 11, 1847. He didn't mind the weather because he knew he'd be knee deep in snow if he were still in Massachusetts. He found an inexpensive but relatively clean lodging house and slept for a whole day.

After taking it easy for a few days, he started looking for work. Stopping in at a tavern along the wharf, he sat at the bar and ordered a whiskey. The man sitting next to him ordered the same and the two men started talking.

Finishing his whiskey, the mans' expression and tenor became slightly more serious as he relayed his story regarding a saw mill that was being built one hundred and forty miles northeast of San Francisco, near the city of Culoma. This man was an agent who had been hired to find workers, and presumed with Harlan's background at the furniture factory he'd be a good candidate. His strong physique was apparent, and his knowledge of the milling and sawing process could be a benefit to the mill.

Harlan, of course, agreed.

After discussing compensation, the agent explained that the steam vessel Sitka was leaving San Francisco on November 28th, sailing up the Sacramento River and docking some forty miles from Culoma.

Several other men had been hired and would also be traveling on the Sitka. The agent was anticipating hiring more men before the twenty-eighth.

Transportation to the mill, once the Sitka docked, had been arranged.

Labor! Harlan didn't want to labor, but realized that this was a good opportunity, and what else could he expect. He still had nearly half of his savings, and this job would enable him to hold on to that reserve, so he agreed to work at the mill.

On the twenty-eighth, he showed up at the wharf

hauling his worn Saratoga trunk containing clothing, rifles, guns, ammunition, and not much else. There was no sentiment in that trunk.

He boarded the Sitka – destination Sutter's Mill.

* * * * * *

It was a cold, crisp, sunny day with no clouds in sight when he arrived in Culoma, California. The day after arriving, he met with James W. Marshall. To both their surprises they had met back in New Jersey years before, and found camaraderie in those experiences. Harlan knew he could use this to his advantage in future endeavors, so consequently he sat patiently in the hard wooden chair seemingly engrossed in what Mr. Marshall was saying.

He listened to the story of Sutter's Mill – how John Sutter, a land developer, hired Marshall because of his carpentry skills to build a water-powered saw mill. The mill was located at the bank of the South Fork American River.

Harlan told Mr. Marshall of his experience at the Heywood-Wakefield Furniture Factory and politely explained that Gardner was the center for lumber and furniture industries back east. Mr. Marshal nodded in agreement. He was well aware of the factory. Furthermore, as was Harlan's nature, he exaggerated his experience in that factories' saw mills.

He went to work the next day. The pay was good and Harlan was satisfied, at least for now. The workers were housed in small but adequate cabins, and true to his nature, Harlan kept to himself.

It's January 24, 1848 and Harlan had been working on

the mill construction for less than two months. Typically it was a no nonsense job, and with little excitement. On this particular day though, he happened to see Mr. Marshall coming back from the field in a frantic mood and hurriedly walking towards Sutter's office. Harlan followed. The office door was slammed shut and Harlan crept to a window and put his ear to the glass. He was hidden by the half drawn curtains.

The conversation was escalating in pitch and fervor as Marshall explained his discovery – his discovery of what he assumed was gold!

Mr. Marshall explained in a frenzied tone that he caught a glimpse of glittering material from the bottom of the river. Picking up a piece of the glittery material, it looked golden, and its shape was half the size of a garden green pea.

He handed a couple of pieces of the supposed gold to Mr. Sutter, who examined the pieces for several minutes. Being familiar with the acid test, and having some of this acid on hand for other uses, he tested the pieces. Sutter gasped and put his hand over his mouth in order to quiet a shriek – high quality gold!

The two men stared at each other and stared some more.

After that, the two men opened the office door, almost taking the door off its hinges, and headed out. Harlan followed clandestinely.

Harlan hid behind a stout tree as he watched the two men kneel down next to the river bank. They kept pulling more and more glittery material from the river. And when they did, the two men yelled feverishly.

It was gold! Harlan had no doubt, as did they, and he knew this was his chance for his fortune. They didn't know he was there and Harlan came up with a plan immediately.

He went to his cabin to get money, and proceeded to the general store, bought food, coffee, blankets, canvas bags, a metal food pan, a shovel, and an oil lamp with extra fuel. Harlan predicted that the store clerk wouldn't be curious as to his purchases, which he wasn't, nor would he mention it to anyone, which he didn't.

He loaded most of the equipment on his back, carrying the rest in his hands, and headed towards the river. He went further upstream of where his bosses discovered the gold.

Kneeling at the river bank, Harlan dredged the river bottom with the pan. Gold nuggets were in the pan with almost every dredge! At this level of reward for his labor, panning the whole night through was not a burden. Newly dredged nuggets and flakes of gold sparkled as the oil lamp was held over the pan.

By the next morning, a whole canvas bag was full of nuggets of varying sizes. Harlan buried this treasure next to a huge oak tree some two hundred feet from the river bank.

Each night Harlan went back to the river for as many hours as his body could tolerate. He knew he couldn't pan during the day because it could draw suspicion as to where he was, and he didn't want to alert anyone as to what he was doing.

Each night Harlan panned in a different spot, always well upstream of Marshall's original discovery. By now he was confident that Sutter and Marshall were trying to keep their discovery hushed. For how long this strategy might work, he had no idea, so he kept at it nightly.

* * * * * *

Four days had passed, and he knew he could amass a fortune in a short period. He dug deep holes around several trees and filled them with the gold, covering the filled holes with rocks and bushes. Time wasn't on his side, and he knew he should pan during the day, as well as at night.

This secret couldn't stay a secret much longer.

Harlan decided to quit the mill.

But before doing so, he secured a heavy-duty wagon with one ox, telling the wagon master that he needed it for hauling rocks, and giving a false name. The wagon master didn't hesitate, and produced the exact size wagon, with one ox, as requested.

Harlan made sure that the wagon and ox were to his satisfaction, and checked the hickory piece protruding from the front of the wagon to ensure that it was well connected to the yoke.

Grabbing hold of the hickory tongue, and walking beside the ox, he thanked the master and headed to the general store. There, he purchased heavy cord, more canvas, and a well-built trunk with a sturdy lock.

After hiding the wagon and walking back to the mill, Harlan found Mr. Marshall and said he was quitting that day, since he needed to be back in San Francisco.

Harlan had cleared a narrow wagon trail a short distance from the camp to his secret location, covering it with branches and leaves to disguise its presence. The trail was arduous, and that's why he chose an ox rather than mules. The ox would be more reliable, easier to manage, and could pull a fully loaded wagon up ravines and through mud holes. And it could get by eating poor grass.

He had no idea as to the final weight of the gold, but knew his ox and wagon would be able to haul all of it.

Arriving at the river he took a piece of bread out of his food basket and sat down while he made a cup of coffee. He sat next to a tree, impressed by his own devices.

Almost three months had passed since getting the wagon, and it was time to head out. Harlan felt lucky no one had seen him. Being careful not to be seen had proved effective. And Sutter's and Marshall's secret evidently was still a secret, at least for now.

He loaded the gold into the trunk and secured it on the wagon. Once that was done, he covered the wagon with a large piece of canvas and tied each end down.

After making sure his cargo was fastened down tightly, he headed out, with his only misgiving being whether or not Sutter had any claim to his gold. If he did, a new plan would be devised. It was Harlan's gold and he'd do anything to keep it.

The ox pulled the wagon with no trouble and Harlan's luck continued when he was told that the Sitka was heading back to San Francisco in a few days. His timing couldn't have been better.

Harlan's wry sneer greeted San Francisco as the Sitka

docked. When he was here last, he was one of those pitiful working class chaps. Not now! He finally was getting the life he deserved.

San Francisco was noticeably different. The docks were empty for the most part.

One crew member was helping Harlan unload his trunk off the Sitka and onto a wagon. Just then, several other crew members were heard shouting "gold, gold at Sutter's Mill!" And they were running frantically in all directions.

The word spread quickly.

Samuel Brannan had run up and down the streets of San Francisco with a bottle of gold supposedly found at Sutter's Mill shouting "gold, gold," and within days most of the men in the city were on their way to find their fortunes.

Harlan knew instantly that this meant his gold was safe from any claim by Sutter or any other entity. It was his to keep and he beat the rush.

Luck had been on his side.

He drove his wagon down the emptying streets. There was madness all around. It appeared everyone in San Francisco was realizing their future – they'd be *rich!*

Harlan had given a lot of thought to what his first, second, and final step should be once he reached San Francisco. Knowing he wanted to go back East, and according to plan, he checked into the same lodging house he stayed at six months prior. He asked and received the room he wanted – the one that allowed the most protection for his gold. The room was visible from the lobby, and it was on the second floor.

Any way you look at it, Harlan pondered, getting the gold back East was risky. Getting robbed was a conceivable outcome. Traveling by wagon train seemed the most precarious.

After some intense analysis, Harlan reasoned that the sea lanes were probably his safest way to travel even after considering the dangers of going around Cape Horn.

Harlan knew that these merchant vessels rarely carried passengers, but believed by offering a sufficient sum of cash (all his saved monies) he'd be able to buy passage – which he did.

No one suspected he had gold in the trunk because the rush was just beginning. And, it wasn't protocol for the crew of a ship to ask what's inside a trunk that boards their vessel.

Even so, Harlan acted the preacher, and complained that he only sold ten of these newly printed bibles, and now had to haul the heavy trunk, laden with the bibles, back east.

To protect his gold further, he made it known that his family was picking him up when they docked in New York. He hoped this would discourage any shenanigans.

CHAPTER 20

AH, TO BE RICH

The trip around the horn and through the Drake Passage was fraught with seasickness, strong winds, and large waves. Five months after leaving San Francisco, the ship docked at the New York City harbor.

Harlan's trunk was loaded onto a wagon and he headed directly to an assayer. The gold needed to be appraised.

The assayer, a jolly plump fellow with pince-nez spectacles that clipped on to the bottom edge of his nose, was patient and took his time examining the gold pieces.

Harlan stood vigilance over his cargo.

Holding a piece of the material, the assayer rubbed it on a black stone leaving a visible mark. Then, he dabbed aqua fortis on the mark and it remained visible.

A satisfying grin crossed his face as he quickly reached for another bottle sitting to his right. Opening that bottle labeled aqua regia, he tested the mark again by applying a small amount of this acid and the mark dissolved. Using differing strengths of the aqua regia, he tested for purity.

He was indeed amazed and astonished at not only the quantity of the gold placed on the table before him, but especially, the quality. After wincing, flinching, and taking deep inhalations, he took off his spectacles, laid them down, and immediately picked them up, putting them back on his nose, while letting out an effusive whoosh.

The jolly fellow was entranced.

When the value of the gold pieces was revealed by the assayer, Harlan's heart almost stopped. This was the first time, and the last time, he was ever at a loss for words.

He was rich!

Not only was he wealthy, but now, he'd never have to put up with anyone telling him what to do. This conclusion was even more pleasing than being rich!

He had visited Philadelphia once and liked the town, and during his ocean voyage, decided to settle there. Early in November, 1848, he read an article in the newspaper about the California gold rush, and beamed with satisfaction.

This pleasing mood was erased as soon as he read further on about the Seneca Falls "Declaration of Rights and Sentiments" document that had been written that past July. Elizabeth Cady Stanton, once again, and her rabid followers! He shook his head with vehement disapproval.

Until recently, women knew their place – their station in life. They're akin to wild horses that must be tamed! Otherwise, these females won't know how to behave as proper women, as proper wives.

As soon as that last thought crossed Harlan's mind, an

inspiration began to take hold. He let that thought stew for a while, and then it came to him, in a flash, just as a small devilish grin replaced the scowl.

A School!

CHAPTER 21

THE HARLAN SCHOOL
FOR YOUNG LADIES

Could he pull it off?

His vision: a school that trains young girls to be attractive, devoted, interesting, and most importantly, obedient wives.

Where to find the girls? Would gentlemen want these trained females? Would they pay for them and wait for them? He had more questions than answers at this point, but he perceived the idea to be brilliant – like himself!

He'd call the school, The Harlan School for Young Ladies, after himself. Why not? It was clearly his idea.

The prospect of this school had Harlan's mind racing with all sorts of possibilities. It kept him up for days.

The answers were coming. And the answers were exactly what he was hoping for. He was beginning to think that this school was not only possible, but probable.

Most importantly, it was needed. Yes. Needed!

This was in fact a civic duty!

Harlan wrote down every tactic, idea, and inspiration that came to mind. He was remembering things from his past that could assist in getting the school to fruition.

The arcade! That would be a great place to observe young girls. Are they pretty, headstrong, malleable?

Observers from the school could direct the girls to various games to test their abilities, their talents.

His girls were going to be beauties, with abilities that set them apart. They'd know how to run the household and servants, entertain guests, and never question their husbands, or their lives.

Each girl would be "groomed" and tailor-made for a particular husband. This way, the man receives his own perfect wife, one designed specifically for him. She'd be an attractive and well behaved wife, having the same likes and dislikes as that particular gentleman. If he liked Bach, so would she. If he wanted her to sing, she'd be delighted to. If his native language was not English, she'd be able to converse in that foreign tongue accurately and promptly.

The process would begin with the school receiving a "Letter of Intention," an agreement from the gentleman that lists the qualifications for his new wife. A price would be negotiated, and the young lady best suited would be picked.

The grooming process would begin.

Harlan decided that thirteen was the best age to start the young girl's development. Depending on the stipulations as set out in the agreement, the school would have three to four years to prepare the young lady for that marriage.

During those years, the gentlemen could observe their particular young lady to ensure his satisfaction.

Harlan knew that the law would not condone his school, and therefore it would be imperative to hide the true nature of its teachings. This, he thought, could be done easily.

Harlan saw no down side to his school, and proceeded to make it a reality.

How many girls would be needed? Where to get them? How many gentlemen would want this service? How would the gentlemen know of the school? He knew he couldn't advertise.

Was the cost tolerable?

Letting the issues simmer, one by one, each question was answered, with a resoundingly positive response. The most important question was answered first. Where to secure young girls? Pay orphanages; pay impoverished or calloused families for their child. One less mouth to feed and they'd have extra money. Benefits to everyone! Harlan was galvanized and the scheme was gaining momentum.

A school for young ladies – a finishing school!

No one outside the school, except the future husbands – the members – would know the truth.

* * * * * *

Harlan bought acreage fifteen miles outside the city of Philadelphia, just far enough away from the city to discourage probing eyes. It was a beautifully treed property, typical for this part of the country, with shrubberies and flowers enhancing the landscape. A large natural pond was positioned so perfectly that Harlan could already see its view from many rooms as he envisioned his school.

Harlan consulted an architect and drew tentative plans for the building. Soon after, the plans were finalized and the construction began in earnest.

Teachers and mentors were essential, each with a specific area of expertise: music, art, or foreign language. Additionally, proper young ladies needed proficiency in the English language, and perhaps a bit of history to round out their education.

Proper dress, etiquette, and the fundamentals of running a household must be part of the curriculum.

The young ladies would be taught to set aside their own wants and desires, in favor of their husband's necessities and private life.

They'd settle into their husband's world.

Harlan knew that the teachers and mentors, for the most part, needed to be men. A woman's influence could damage his product. And besides, they might see through the veil of the school's true purpose. With men, he could tell them the truth, and use them as needed. Several have already agreed to work at The Harlan School, each one agreeing that the true purpose of the school was absolutely an exceptional idea – a vision demanded for these changing times.

Each would act as an agent and locate gentlemen interested in securing a future wife. Before long, Harlan would have full time agents, with a plethora of agreements.

The cooks and other general help ought to be men too. Harlan was sure of this. And he knew a local doctor who already agreed to be on staff in order to answer the girl's personal issues and general health concerns.

One problem remained – the work done by chambermaids, housemaids, scullery maids, and of course, ladies maids. No different than a well-run household, these maids are imperative in order to ensure that the Harlan young ladies focus strictly on becoming the obedient wives of wealthy gentlemen. These Harlan ladies will be running households, not doing the menial work.

Maids were typically women or young girls. It's inconceivable that young boys could do these jobs without creating major difficulties and distractions. It should be easy to get young girls, say eleven to thirteen, for these maids. At that young age they'd be easily trainable, and taught not to question what they were told. They might stay on for years or be dismissed for any number of reasons. He could get them from orphanages and from destitute families, same as he could get prospective Harlan young ladies.

Except, no matter where they were from, the selection of these future maids would be based on a very different standard than the future wives.

The "maid standard" would specify an extremely shy and homely young girl. They'd be no competition for the Harlan young ladies. After all, the Harlan young ladies would be beauties. These young girls, though hand-picked too, would not be.

Who would govern them? Who would keep them in line? Who would know to dispose of them if they caused any trouble? In a private household, a housekeeper is in charge of the maids. Where to find a housekeeper who wouldn't see through the veil of the school, or wouldn't care if she did? Perhaps there was a woman who, for the right price, could do the job, with no questions asked, no matter what she observed?

She'd be proficient in directing and training maids, and would know women's clothing and styling. And, ideally, she'd know a couple of women who, for the right price, would help teach these feminine necessities with the same attitude.

After some time, Harlan eventually resolved this issue of finding the right housekeeper by a recollection. He remembered a woman he'd met years before while living in New Jersey. Harlan had caught her stealing, and her lack of empathy for what she had done intrigued him. He had let her go without notifying the authorities.

She was a stout and rather unattractive woman with strong arms and nerves of steel. A disdain for society was apparent in her demeanor and actions, and a kinship between she and Harlan, it seemed, could easily develop.

He remembered that she had worked as a chambermaid, and later worked in her husband's shop as a seamstress, and a considerably good one at that.

Unfortunately, the husband let the drink take away their livelihood.

What was her name?

Did it not start with a "T"?

Tryon! Yes. Mrs. Tryon.

First name – what was it?

Priscilla? Patsy? No.

Yes, yes. Patience! Patience Tryon.

How could he forget that name? This woman appeared to be anything but patient.

Just before heading west, Harlan met a patron of the cigar shop who knew the Tryons, and reported that Mr. Tryon had died a year earlier and that Mrs. Tryon had been struggling as a seamstress and a mid-wife.

Harlan had promised if he ever had a place for her, in any endeavor, he'd find her. They both knew it was an empty promise. Today, it wasn't. After hiring a detective to track her down, she agreed immediately to come to Harlan's school. She'd be the Housekeeper, in full charge of the maids. Housekeeping duties would be light, allowing her to teach etiquette and styling, along with the two women she would bring with her.

All was in place and the school opened.

CHAPTER 22

THEIR CONVERSATION

He walked into a tavern one night, and recognized a man sitting alone at a table. At first, he couldn't recall why he knew this man. Nonetheless, as acute as a lightning strike, Harlan remembered. Dorsey! Harlan hadn't thought of him for years. The last time he saw Dorsey, he was falling out of the foundry breaking his ankle.

Harlan had now made his fortune from gold, and his school was running smoothly and making money. Unlike the first time he met Dorsey, now he wore the latest fashion – a dark grey morning coat with black velvet trim. Harlan looked distinguished, and he knew it.

Dorsey looked haggard.

Harlan told the bartender he'd like to buy a drink for the man sitting at the table below the window – the one draped with the heavy curtains, which mirrored Dorsey's demeanor, Harlan noted.

"Whatever he is drinking… double it," he added with a cynical charm.

The bartender put a tumbler of whiskey in front of the

gentlemen sitting at that table, and told him it was from the gentleman sitting at the end of the bar. Dorsey was grateful and focused his eyes on the man that was so generous. He thought he'd recognize him, but didn't. Not at first.

The man smiled at Dorsey and something was familiar, almost too familiar. A sick feeling developed in the pit of his stomach and he knew immediately who this man was.

Nathaniel Dorsey was now wishing he hadn't walked into this tavern. It was next to the inn where he was spending the night. He could have made it home by dark but the extra time away was too tempting.

He refused the drink and got up to leave when, without warning, Harlan was in front of him, blocking the way to the outside door.

"Do not say you do not remember me!" Harlan wisecracked with a sneered expression.

"Let us sit down and enjoy our whiskey – talk over old times – see how things are going now," Harlan added with a hint of mockery.

Dorsey observed that this nemesis was dressed in the finest of the days' fashion, which would have demanded a high price.

From a lowly farrier to this! What circumstances could have aided this transformation? He was not amused.

Dorsey's business was in dire straits and his meeting in Boston did not go well. He received only a small portion of the capital his company needed. It was enough for a short while, but not enough for even the near future. He was sitting in this tavern contemplating his next move.

Unfortunately, options were limited and the whiskey was not.

Sitting back down, Dorsey drank the whiskey while Harlan sat in the chair next to him, raising a glass for a toast.

"Come on Dorsey, a toast. Let the old days be forgotten and let us toast to better years ahead!"

Harlan swallowed his whiskey in one gulp and immediately ordered two more.

"You are looking rather pensive," Harlan expressed as if Dorsey would be surprised by this observation. Dorsey said nothing and took a large swig of the whiskey placed before him as he scrutinized Harlan in disbelief and contempt. Here was the man that changed his life forever, and by all appearances, this vile and undeserving man, had more money than himself.

It was easy for Dorsey to see that a little friendliness at this juncture might stop any future torment from this fellow. There was no way to know if he'd run into him again someday. And a modicum of conversation could alleviate the strain of this days' unwanted encounter. So he spoke of his ordeal after the "incident" in that small town so many years ago. The ankle never healed well, and a distinctive limp was his persistent memento. It stopped him from riding horses and stopped him cold in his profession.

He had owned land, that was true, but the land needed a strong hand to govern, not a weakened man. Selling the land, he moved his family further north, a few miles from

Boston.

There he opened a small factory with the remnants of the monies from the land sale, and it prospered and grew throughout the years.

A new competitor had come onto the market place and was building and selling his product cheaper. The only way to compete was to upgrade his factory which took capital, which he didn't have. He was sitting here, in this tavern, thinking about all the banks that turned down his request for that needed cash.

Harlan listened intently, and heard opportunities in Dorsey's every word. In an instant, a grudge could be satisfied with Dorsey's total dependence on Harlan.

Meeting back at the tavern the following day, Harlan agreed to give Dorsey the needed capital. In exchange for Harlan's generosity, Dorsey would use his connections to obtain clients for the school. Through his business dealings Dorsey knew not only the upper crust of the northeast and central states, but also knew many aristocratic foreign gentlemen and families.

That Harlan Leighton had this kind of money caused Dorsey to become suspicious, and as Harlan explained the source of his wealth, jealousy engulfed Dorsey – gold! Needing to be judicious, he put aside his angst and listened to Harlan's proposal, at first with amusement, and then with total attentiveness.

As he listened to Harlan, he was in disbelief regarding the true intention of the school and expected it to be a joke. He soon realized that Harlan was serious, as was the school.

Dorsey did not want to go home the day before for several reasons, principally because of his wife. She had changed and no longer gave him a peaceful home. Could this school actually produce dutiful and obedient wives – wives made to order? Hmmm, intriguing, but, was this ethical?

After giving Dorsey time to think, Harlan prompted him for a response. He knew that Dorsey was desperate and trusted that the desperation would create a loyal follower. Harlan was an excellent judge of character, and Dorsey was ripe for exploitation.

Dorsey needed the money; he couldn't see an alternative when there was none. After a short pause to consolidate his decision, Dorsey looked directly into Harlan's shrewd eyes, and said "Yes."

CHAPTER 23

HIS DESCENDANTS

"Leighton. That is what he said his name was," the young man exclaimed enthusiastically, in a high pitched voice.

"Could he be your relative?" he inquired.

Aaron had been told that Mr. Leighton did not have any relatives and thought this might be good news for him – conceivably, these Leighton's could be long lost family members.

Harlan was puzzled. He stroked his mustache and finally asked "Where did you say you met him?"

"In Harrisburg while I was learning about the local families for the upcoming bazaar. He lives on a small farm outside town, has two young sons and a wife. She is quite a beauty!" Aaron professed with the manner of a school boy's crush.

"On the day I went to Church to observe the families, Mrs. Leighton sang a hymn. Her voice is as beautiful as she is.

And you were right, Mr. Leighton. These people are aching for a distraction from the war – it has been too close to their daily lives. Gettysburg at least was forty miles away, but the skirmish the month before at Sporting Hill, was just two miles west of Harrisburg! I think our timing could not be better," he declared grinning.

Harlan agreed that this city was "ripe for the pickings," and then assured Aaron that the Harrisburg Leighton's couldn't be related as he had no living relatives. He even feigned disappointment.

All day he ruminated. Could it be? Harlan didn't want to ever see his son again, but he was curious.

The next day he boarded the train and was off to Harrisburg.

* * * * * *

There he was – his son! He was easily recognizable save the limp. And his right arm had been amputated. Harlan assumed that these impairments were the result of serving as a soldier in the war. Years earlier, Harlan had paid the government a hefty price ($300 per head) to keep himself and his teachers and mentors out of the war. Of course these gentlemen gradually paid Harlan back through their earned wages at the school – a small price to pay for keeping their lives intact.

The son's farm was visibly meager, to say the least, and it must have been difficult to feed a family of four. Watching his son always at a distance merely satisfied Harlan's curiosity. There was no paternal connection – no paternal fondness or tenderness.

The son's reputation, Harlan determined, was appalling. And he saw no comparison to his own. At that moment his arrogance conveniently negated his own past behaviors.

Today, Harlan considered himself an established and respectable citizen. Such a person as himself must portray an honorable representation to everyone. His son, evidently, did not learn this societal constraint.

He hadn't seen his son's wife until one afternoon in town. This young woman was walking out of the linen shop and when she crossed Harlan's path, her beauty was overpowering. He had seen beautiful women before, of course, but there was something extraordinary about this woman. You could fathom her grueling life, yet, her face nevertheless was angelic, with a smile that would soften even the hardest of beasts. Her eyes were like emeralds and sparkled akin to the most expensive gemstone. She offered the sweetest "Good Afternoon" to the passerby's and Harlan's heart was assuaged.

Who was that woman, he asked a passerby. And when he was told who she was, he was in unmitigated disbelief.

It couldn't be.

This was his son's wife! How did that union take place?

Harlan didn't like women typically, as he viewed them as rather useless creatures except to bear children. But this woman, for whatever cause, drew him in. He couldn't stop thinking about her. Was it strictly because she was his son's wife? Forbidden fruit, so to speak?

Harlan's moral compass never pointed in any particular direction and believed the premise of forbidden fruit was nonsense. If you want something, anything, take it.

From what Harlan had learned about his son's antics, he mistreated his wife persistently.

Harlan laughed over his concern for this woman. Was this the first time he cared about the weaker sex? Yes, it assuredly was. And here he was infatuated with a woman he did not even know.

Did not even know! As soon as the phrase entered his mind, he knew it was essential for him to get to know her.

He'd pretend to be someone else not allowing her to know their actual relationship. His son could never know Harlan had wealth. If he did, he could enter Harlan's life and make demands. More importantly, he could claim the school as the heir apparent. That wouldn't be allowed! Harlan hadn't considered so far what would happen to the school after his death. He precisely knew it was not to go to his son, of all people.

Harlan decided to stay in Harrisburg for a few months and before long cultivated a relationship with his son's wife. She seemed to appreciate the times they shared together. Their talks were of interesting topics, not mundane gossip or chatter. They'd meet in tea rooms or restaurants, or walk along the banks of the Susquehanna River. Harlan always acted the gentlemen and their bond grew with no indication of any impropriety. She believed he was in Harrisburg for these few months closing a business transaction and was desperate for conversation.

If Harlan was capable of love, this was that moment. He adored this woman with a passion he had never felt before. It was gratifying and he didn't want to let go.

One day he decided to ask her to marry him, and to

his absolute astonishment, she refused. At first he imagined it must be because of the child she was now bearing – his son's child. But she refused because she didn't love him.

He was offering this female and the unborn child the world and it wasn't enough! How *dare* she not accept his proposal – the impertinence, the audacity!

Harlan was surprised at his own fury, and as that resentment took hold, he assured himself that she wouldn't live long enough to hold her newborn baby. A plan for her demise was brewing, and it would be carried out – no going back – his pride demanded it!

CHAPTER 24

FIXATION

Aaron had completed and filed all the necessary paperwork and permits in order for the bazaar to open. It had been thirteen years since the bazaar re-visited Harrisburg. He always wondered why the school never went back there, and Harlan's reason was nothing more than a pat response that wasn't satisfactory. Knowing better, Aaron never pressed for more information.

Harlan had always been the one to decide where to open the bazaar, but lately he passed that decision onto Aaron and was quite satisfied with the results. He knew he was being juvenile and impractical regarding his lingering obsession with that woman and lifted the ban on Harrisburg.

Upon his return from Harrisburg, Aaron produced a list of prospective schoolgirls, and as Harlan was reviewing the details, Aaron offered news of the Leighton family.

Sitting at his desk stoically, Harlan listened.

"Remember me telling you that I thought they might

be relatives of yours? Well, the mother died in childbirth, and the family's conditions are as dire, if not more so, than they were thirteen years ago.

And there is a thirteen year old girl who is the exact image of the mother. Once you have seen that woman, you do not easily forget her. I think *this* young girl would fit in well at Harlan. There are other girls in Harrisburg who fit our bill, but this young girl, I think, is exceptional.

A real beauty!

I go back next week to make arrangements for the young girls to attend the bazaar."

As Harlan was nodding approvingly, Aaron quieted, stood up, and took his leave.

Harlan stayed seated and was surprised by his reaction to Aarons update: excitement.

A daughter! He hadn't thought of her child, never did, and now she'd be going to the bazaar. Did she really look like her mother? Was her personality similar? Harlan decided to be present at the Harrisburg bazaar and watch, watch for her.

* * * * * *

He coveted her mother, he knew this, and after seeing the daughter, wanted to covet her. Harlan knew this child was not the woman he met thirteen years ago, but this women's child would remind him of the only connection he ever felt for another human being. This child was an uncultivated, untamed young girl and would have to develop and mature before he'd have her in his life – he wanted a young woman, not a child. Waiting a few years would be no problem.

This was, after all, the tenant of the school: cultivated young ladies, virgins.

Scrutinizing this young girl at the bazaar, Harlan was confident that she was her mother's daughter, both in appearance and temperament, never seeing any of his son's erratic behavior in her actions.

The indication of an incestuous fascination would never cross Harlan's mind. She was simply "her" daughter – nothing more.

In time, she'd be his. And he had time. He was in no rush and as the years progressed, he watched and observed her clandestinely.

He signed the typical Harlan School agreement strictly to ensure that she'd not be sold to anyone else. He knew mistakes occur, and he wasn't going to lose her to some bureaucratic error because of some verbal misunderstanding.

She would be his wife.

PART III A FINE YOUNG WOMAN

CHAPTER 25

KNOWING

It's been six months since her birthday party celebrating her seventeen years of life. Lacey's all grown up, regal in appearance and character, and stunning.

This sophisticated and versatile young lady sings like an angel, recites poetry with the proper emotion and intonation, appreciates art from the masters, plays the three types of harpsichords and the fortepiano with ease, is fluent in French and Italian, could run a household perfectly, and understands the duties of a wife and mother.

Lacey is the quintessential Harlan young lady.

Waking up this morning, she got out of bed, put on her robe, and started to get ready for the day.

The matching ewer and wash basin stood ready on the table stand waiting to be used. They were made of porcelain, with tiny red and yellow rosebuds adorning the outer edges. Lacey poured the warm water into the basin, wetted a soft velvet cloth, and washed herself gently, as she had done for so many years.

The young lady finished dressing, thanked the ladies maid, and was smiling as she reminisced over the past year since her birthday. There had been no difficulties nor any doubts, and no apprehension. The last episode was a week after her birthday, and there hadn't been one of those incidences since. She had put all those imaginings behind her.

Not having a suitor, as did the other seventeen year olds was no longer a concern. She'd be on her own if that was her destiny, and she'd be prepared for that.

The school had given her the confidence to venture beyond these safe walls, to find adventures wherever they lay. Teaching at a young ladies finishing school was a good way for her to earn a living. She had learned invaluable skills at Harlan that she could pass onto other young girls.

She considered the possibility of teaching at Harlan, if they would allow that, but her heart was set on gaining new experiences. Staying at Harlan seemed too sheltered.

And someday perhaps, she'd meet the right gentleman.

She adjusted the pins holding the curled bun sitting precisely to the left of her nape, and opened the door. Heading to the dining room, she was especially hungry. Perhaps her good mood was the reason.

Virtually floating down the hallway, Lacey could smell the sweet cinnamon buns wafting towards her. She smiled as she remembered her first bun at the bazaar so many years before. Rarely does she think of those days.

Lacey never did develop a close friendship with any of the girls at Harlan – not since Rueby left without a good bye or explanation. She told herself that she'd never let another heartbreak like that happen again. It saddened her tremendously but she knew that once she left the school, true friendships would come into her life. In the meantime, she enjoyed acquaintances with her classmates, nothing more.

Walking into the dining room, she saw an empty chair at the far right of the room. Sitting at that same table, were the two young ladies Lacey discerned as being sad and solemn girls. She never understood their uneasiness. As far as Lacey had observed, they were the only ones to have this disposition.

These were the same girls she had seen two years earlier walking up the stairs with pained expressions. Do they know something she doesn't know? Whenever this thought crossed her mind, as was her habit, she'd immediately reprimand herself for falling back to her old suspicious and unreasonable ways.

They were a year older than Lacey, and whenever she had an opportunity to speak with them, their responses were brisk or fleeting. It wasn't a rudeness Lacey believed, but rather a lack of interest in her personally. All the same, she held no acrimony and was always pleasant.

These two young ladies would only be at the school for another month. Adelia and Prudence were getting married.

They both had been at the school much longer than any of the other young ladies. At Harlan School, when a young lady turned seventeen (and possibly fifteen or sixteen) she'd leave Harlan, to get married.

Lacey, along with Adelia and Prudence, evidently were the exceptions.

She enjoyed sitting at the table in front of the picture window. From that vantage point she could look out onto the picturesque pond and with sheer delight watch the various kinds of birds – some large, others smaller with innumerable colored feathers. The reflections of the trees surrounding the pond added to the splendor.

It was a beautiful sunny morning, the day had just begun, and there was so much to look forward to.

Abruptly, the outside door, opposite the picture window, flew open with a thunderous crash. The room became quiet except for the voice of one girl crying, which could be heard above the sound of her swift footsteps landing hard on the wood floor. Lacey turned around in time to see the girl collapse next to the fire hearth. Her dress was torn and dirty, her face bruised, her hair pulled out of its delicately pinned bun. She was shivering and shuddering.

No one in the room was moving.

Lacey couldn't understand this aloof behavior, and as she was rising from her chair to help this panicked young girl, the two young ladies sitting across from her leapt up in unison. Adelia hastily dashed around the table, put her hands on Lacey's shoulders, and fiercely put her back down in her seat.

Before Lacey could react to this brute force, teachers and mentors came streaming in through the doors and positioned themselves at the tables to soothe the girls.

"Be calm, please. Everything is all right. Do not worry.

This young lady was traveling outside the school to Philadelphia to see the doctor when her carriage was attacked by thieves. We will take good care of her," their voices proclaimed.

All the girls and the young ladies were relieved, except the young ladies sitting by the picture window.

Two footmen took the disheveled girl away.

Lacey was frantic and asked Adelia and Prudence if they knew what was going on. She firmly believed they knew something. And she didn't believe the story about the thieves. They both looked at her incredulously and put their finger to their lips, "shhh."

It was obvious that they didn't want to draw attention to themselves. Adelia, whose intensity was in stark contrast to her best friends' even-temperament quietly whispered, "You really do not know what is going on?"

Lacey shook her head and said in a whispered tone,

"No, I do not."

And then, Adelia and Prudence both looked directly at Lacey and said in unison, "You are promised to Harlan!"

Harlan! The school? Lacey had no idea what they were talking about.

Promised to the school?

"Leighton! Harlan Leighton! Do you not know who he is?" Prudence said in a quivering voice with tears welling in pained eyes. "He owns this school, and he owns you – Lacey Leighton!" she promptly declared.

Immediately Lacey's heart and head began to throb. She could feel the rush of blood flushing her face.

"Harlan Leighton? He owns me and the school? How?

Am I related to him? Why have I not met him? I never heard his name before," Lacey whispered with rising panic.

Looking around the room to make sure no one was listening, Adelia recounted, in a strained voice, how she and Prudence had been exploring the school a short time after arriving at Harlan.

"It was late one night and everyone was sleeping. We were walking the stairs when we decided to play hide and seek. After a while we found ourselves at the entrance to the guest's wing. In front of us was a locked double door. But that was not going to stop our fun because I can pick just about any lock – something I learned from my thieving brothers.

Hair pins work for picking locks, so I took two pins out of my hair. The lock was easy to pick and we went into the wing. Everything was quiet. We found ourselves in the dining room, and explored this part of the building. It was there we saw the life-size painting of Harlan Leighton. His name was inscribed on a brass plate at the bottom of the frame.

It was getting late. We worried we might wake someone, so we returned to the dormitory."

Pausing, Adelia took a deep breath.

Little did she know that her proficiency in picking locks would confirm the reality of their nightmare.

Peering directly at Lacey, Prudence, sobbing and fidgeting with her curly tresses, wanted to tell Lacey the rest of the story, but was too frightened. Adelia took hold of Prudence's hand and hastily unveiled the rest of their story.

"One night, a year after seeing the painting, we could not sleep and we decided to play hide and seek on the floors below so as to not wake anyone – we wanted to avoid the guest's wing.

I was trying to find a suitable hiding place, when I stopped in front of Mr. Olson's office door.

'A great place to hide,' I thought and picked the lock. It was effortless.

I ducked into the office and waited for Prudence to find me. There were papers lying in the middle of the desk. I put my lamp down and started reading the papers.

Each had a heading that read 'The Harlan School for Young Ladies – Letter of Intent' and stated monies to be exchanged for a wife – a wife with specific traits which were listed one by one.

The letter of intent was signed by 'Harlan Leighton' and the 'Member – Husband.'

Harlan Leighton! I remembered that name – the man in the painting!

I knew immediately that hide and seek was over."

Taking another deep breath, Adelia scrutinized Lacey to see her reaction.

Lacey was astonished at what she just heard. Could this all be true? Her heart was sinking.

Adelia continued.

"I ran down the hall to find Prudence and to tell her what I had read. Then we sat on the floor in the hall next to our room and cried as soundlessly as we could.

We both knew our fate.

We seriously thought about running away or telling someone, but where to go, and who would take us seriously? Would our lives be in danger?"

Tears welled in Adelia's eyes and she swiped them away with defiance.

"This Harlan Leighton is a ghost. No one ever sees him or talks about him. But we saw his picture in the painting, and it is a face you do not forget."

A moment of silence passed, and Lacey listened in horror as Adelia, softly and quietly intimated, "There was a letter on the desk that had to do with you, Lacey Leighton, and, Harlan Leighton as Member – Husband."

But before Lacey could ask Adelia and Prudence any more questions, Lacey watched as each of the young ladies simultaneously lowered their heads and began to tremble.

She watched as their whole bodies withdrew and wilted in their chairs.

"What is going on?" she asked frantically.

More silence, and a few seconds passed.

Then, abruptly, Lacey felt powerful and sturdy hands grasp her shoulders and squeeze tightly.

Terrified, she instinctively turned her head to see whose hands were gripping her shoulders.

A bright glimmer caught her eye. The glimmer was a ring, a gold ring, in the shape of a horseshoe, with diamonds and bright hues dancing to the light.

It couldn't be!

She stared at the ring with utter disbelief, and felt faint. The room was suddenly cold, and as Lacey looked around, all was in slow motion. The sensibility she possessed could not ease the reality of this moment, and she watched as her memories solidified.

Now, she knew exactly who was behind her.

He was here all along.

Harlan. Grandfather!

Mother, oh Mother, help me!!

EPILOGUE

FOUR YEARS LATER

THE INHERITANCE

The room was filled with the sweet scent of lilacs. They'd been cut from the lilac tree that stood in the garden, and placed in the ornate china vase that sat on the side board. This was a typical Victorian room indicative of those Victorian times, with stark formality, characteristic of the well-to-do.

The powerfully built furniture was made of dark mahogany with tiny lion heads carved into the corners of the side pieces. A long and massive dining table sat in the middle of the room with its complementary silk upholstered chairs. Above was an exquisite chandelier sparkling of crystals and twenty four karat gold.

Colors and hues in the dining room were deep shades of reds and purples with amber trim, and the walls were papered with large floral designs with intricate damask. Two sizeable paintings hung on each side of the room, each with substantial and elaborately carved wood frames. The sun's rays spilled into the room from the picture window overlooking the lushness of the well maintained garden.

The three gentlemen sitting at the table were no strangers. They knew each other well, and had for many years. Each was very different from the other in general appearance, education, and family background.

One gentleman, Doctor Thaddeus Whitaker, was a prominent surgeon, of substantial means, who had enjoyed an outstanding and full-filling life. He was respected by all who knew him. He'd come from a wealthy family, a family of doctors and surgeons, and like his father before him, after years of first-rate surgeries, had become the presiding surgeon at one of the country's most prestigious hospitals.

Sitting directly across from the doctor was his charming, lovely, and dutiful wife. A woman of striking beauty, with a name to match her charms: Damaris.

She sat there with excellent posture, and for most of the time, stayed silent.

To the doctor's right was the sole owner of a cotton textile factory in New England, Mr. Algernon Dorsey, who inherited the business from his father. The son always thought his father a weak and sullied man. This son was nothing like his father. This son's vigor, drive, and tenacity were his strengths.

Mr. Dorsey's outwardly virtuous and accomplished life was marred only by the unsolved murder of his eldest son, many years ago.

His wife wasn't in attendance this evening. Leaving her home was the usual practice.

The third gentleman couldn't boast of these familial

advantages but was now sitting at this table with the power and wealth to make or break gentlemen such as these. And he was always willing and enthusiastic to utilize that power.

Earlier that day, these gentlemen met in the library, where antique, innovative, and contemporary books were housed on shelves lining the walls, reaching to the ceiling. Overstuffed chairs sat waiting for a reader to discover the wonders of these books. And tall brass ladders stood ready for anyone to climb and discover further the pleasures above their heads.

Library books wouldn't be read this afternoon. Instead, the three men in the library were there strictly to discuss the expectations and requirements of the newest patrons to the school, and to determine how many young girls would be required for that fall's attendance.

As was typical of Harlan Leighton, this meeting was clandestine. Not trusting gossip or prying eyes and ears, the three men told no one of this meeting, except the two wives present at the house. The men thought that these two women, of course, had no idea what the meeting was about.

How wrong they were.

The Harlan School's success rate was high and the three gentlemen took immense pride in this achievement. The men were satisfied that less than four percent of their girls, over the years, had to be eliminated.

This was well within their tolerable failure rate.

Of fervent concern was that no one would be able to hear the conversations that took place in the library – a valuable lesson that had been learned years before. This concern was easily addressed: exceptionally thick walls and a heavy door with solid and sturdy locks.

This was Harlan's library and private sanctuary, and no one was allowed admittance unless Harlan was present.

Sitting in one corner of the library was Harlan's massive desk, which held his many secrets.

Another well-kept secret, so Harlan believed, was the hidden passageway. The architect had been paid handsomely to tell no one of its existence.

Concluding their business, the three gentlemen looked forward to the evening meal. After a short while a footman entered the library asking the gentlemen to follow him to the dining room. Dinner was ready.

After the gentleman took their seats, a footman filled their wine glasses and served the first course. After nearly two hours of culinary pleasures and informal conversation, it was time for dessert.

In the kitchen sliced fruit of perfect ripeness was placed on gold-rimmed Lenox china dessert plates. Various types of nuts were overflowing from a matching bowl. Each was placed on a silver serving platter.

Along with the dessert, three glass tumblers appeared on the same serving tray.

As the footman was placing the desserts and the tumblers in front of each gentleman, and removing their empty claret glasses, Damaris, the surgeon's wife, prompted a toast. She held up her glass of warm claret, as each gentleman raised their tumbler and toasted to The Harlan School. As she gently sipped the claret, each gentleman tasted the tumbler's sweet liquid.

The snifter was delicious, unusual, and they each inquired as to what it was.

"A newly discovered concoction, called Godfrey's Cordial. I cannot remember the ingredients, but is it not delightful?" Damaris sweetly replied.

The three gentlemen nodded their heads in approval and continued to drink the delectable nectar.

After finishing the fruit, and the first of three Godfrey's Cordial each, the footman cleared the table, and went back to the kitchen through the swinging door.

During the brief time when the swinging door was ajar, a quick and keen look would have caught sight of a figure standing on the far side of the door, almost blending into the hardness and cold steel of the kitchen.

The figure was that of a woman, impeccably and exquisitely dressed in a vibrant violet gown. A striking diamond broach was pinned to her lace bodice and equally stunning diamond earrings hung from her lobes. Her hair was swept up with a violet ribbon intertwined.

Yet, the woman had a dispirited and toughened face, too dejected and hardened for her age of only twenty-one years. Her shoulders that once rose high and proud were now drooped, lifeless, and so too was her facial expression. No twinkle in those eyes. That light was shut out long ago, leaving a cold and distant presence in this shattered figure.

Clenched tightly in her left hand was a crumpled piece of paper and an envelope, dated years earlier, addressed to Harlan Leighton from Algernon Dorsey.

The note was discovered in a desk drawer some months earlier. The note's single passage read:

I have sent a note to Thaddeus telling

him that Zachary has been eliminated,

and is no longer a threat to us, or the school.

Algernon

Why keep this note after all these years? Was it saved as a form of blackmail, a way to keep two gentlemen in line?

In the woman's right hand was a glass vial, held close to her side. She delicately stroked the vial with her index finger, as if it were a cherished possession.

The vial had a small white label with careless writing:

Sydenham's Laudanum

From their positions on either side of the swinging door, the eyes of two women met in recognition. A supreme and absolute understanding passed between them.

This was their day, a very long time coming. The note found was simply the catalyst for this desperate undertaking.

A scheme had been devised to deliver a fatal dose of a sweet liquid that would stop the school's wretchedness – it was the only resolution, the only way out.

A faint smile crept across the twenty-one year old's face, and when she became aware of this incipient joy, the smile grew stronger. How long had it been since she had cause to smile? She couldn't remember. Smiles had not been abundant in this house; joy had been non-existent. Yet now, the glimmer of incipient joy could be seen intensifying to a glowing radiance from the eyes of Lacey Leighton.

* * * * * *

A Short time later:

Obituary – Boston

Algernon Dorsey, owner of the Dorsey Cotton and Textile Factory, died while out of town on business. He leaves behind his wife and two children. The funeral will be held at the St. Luke's Church this Saturday.

Obituary – New York City

On June 7, Mr. Thaddeus Whitaker died quietly at his home. Mr. Whitaker was a renowned surgeon and is survived by his wife, Damaris, and their two children.

Obituary – Philadelphia

Harlan Leighton died peacefully in his sleep this past Tuesday. He opened the successful Harlan School for Young Ladies. The Harlan School will now be owned and operated by his wife, Lacey Leighton.

The End